JUST ONE NIGHT

Castleton Hearts, Book One

CHELSEA M. CAMERON

Get a Free Book and Stories!

Tropetastic romance with a twist, Happily Ever Afters guaranteed! You can expect humor and heart in every Chelsea M. Cameron romance.

Get access to a free book, free stories, and free bonus chapters! Join Chelsea's Newsletter for bonus content, receive a free ebook, get access to future exclusive bonus material, news, and discounts.

About Just One Night

Paige Roman is out for revenge. Not just any revenge; she's out to mend her recently shattered heart. Her ex, Wyatt, is going to pay, and the best way to make that happen is to seduce the girl he's always wanted but has never caught: Esme Bell. To be fair, the dark-haired bartender with the infectious laugh is the girl just about everyone wants, and Wyatt is no exception.

Paige's plan is simple, and it's going to work. Go out with Esme, take her home, and then rub her victory in Wyatt's face for the whole town of Castleton, Maine to see. She does reconnaissance at the bar where Esme works, and soon, the game is O.N.

Is Paige just going to head right for the bedroom? No. She's more subtle than that. Paige has never really seduced anyone like this, but how hard could it be? She's not completely devoid of sexy skills.

What starts as a plot to get back at her ex turns into something a whole lot more complicated when Paige catches major feelings. Is she ready to give up her mission and put her heart on the line again? Or should she just cut her losses and call the whole thing off?

Chapter One

It wasn't originally my idea. Emerald came up with it, which was strange, considering that it was her own brother that I planned on fucking over.

She leaned over the scarred wooden table between us at the coffee shop. "Think about it. He is obsessed with her. Has been since middle school. *Obsessed.*" Her eyes went wide and I believed her. I mean, he'd tried hitting on her when we were together, which should have been a red flag, but ignoring red flags had become my hobby when I started dating Wyatt.

"How come you're willing to help me get him like this?" I asked. Em and I had been friends since before Wyatt and I started dating, and even though he had broken up with me, we hadn't stopped hanging out. Sure, it was a little weird at first, but she'd let me know if it came to choosing me or him, she'd choose me. Didn't say much about Wyatt's strengths as a brother, did it? He also hadn't been strong as a boyfriend, but I'd been too dazzled by his abs and his smile and the way he'd said all the right things to care at the time. He also gave amazing head, which definitely had something to do with it. I'd hand over all my common sense in exchange for great sex.

"I know I love him because he's my brother and everything, but he's a complete asshole and it's time someone told him that he can't have everything he wants. Plus, I have revenge experience."

That she did. When Em found out her ex had cheated on her, she'd managed to have her car impounded. I'd stopped her from any further sabotage, but I had to admit, it sounded really satisfying.

I sipped at my iced mocha latte. Wyatt had definitely gotten what he wanted from me before he decided he was done and broke up with me in a text message. A message in which he'd used emojis. It wasn't cheating on me, but he'd treated me like trash nonetheless. I'd thought that we were headed for a serious commitment, had planned my future with him, and then he dropped me. Like I didn't even matter. I'd thought I was going to share his name and his life, and I was left with nothing.

She pushed her curly brown hair over her shoulder. "He's gotten every girl he's ever wanted. Except Esme."

Esme. Esme Bell.

"He asked her out in front of me once. He was drunk, and she turned him down, but I wonder how many other times he's asked," I said.

Emerald gave me a look.

"How many times have you seen him ask her out?"

She laughed and shoved the last bite of her croissant in her mouth. "I mean, are we counting the times he straight up asked her to fuck him, or the times when he tried to buy her a drink at her own bar?" Esme was the most-beloved bartender at the only drinking establishment in our small Maine seaside town.

"I can't believe I dated someone so gross."

"Hey, he's my brother. I'm the one who has to share DNA with him." She made a face.

I'd shared plenty of things with Wyatt, but I didn't need to talk about it in front of his sister.

"So, it's simple: seduce Esme and rub it in his face. Oh, and make sure I'm there to see it. I want to treasure that moment in my days to come, and you will too. It'll be worth it." She gazed off into the distance, a smile on her face.

It would be pretty great to see the guy who shattered my heart get his comeuppance. As much as I wanted to deny that I'd just been having fun with him, and it hadn't been serious, I'd given him my foolish heart and now I couldn't get it back. The thing that lived in my chest now was a sad, broken thing. Getting back at him might not mend it, but it would definitely make me feel better.

Emerald took our plates and cups up to the counter and stuck them in the bucket to be washed. I stood up and brushed crumbs off my lap.

"Okay, I'm in. I mean, it's not like it'll be a hardship, sleeping with Esme." Just saying her name felt like I was savoring something delicious in my mouth. It didn't hurt that she was also hot as fuck.

"Mmm, I know, right?" Emerald said, wiggling her eyebrows. She and I had also bonded by being out in our small town.

"I thought she wasn't your type?" I asked.

"I mean, she's not, but I'd let her top me if I was in the right mood."

I'd let her top me in any mood, I thought.

"Let's go scope her out," Emerald said as we both walked toward our respective cars. I paused and fiddled with my keys.

"You want to do what now?"

Emerald grinned and leaned on her car. "Let's go check her out. Formulate a plan."

"Right now?"

"You got something better to do?"

I thought about that for a second. "Other than my like, five jobs, no."

"Great! Let's go."

I sputtered for a second before getting in my car and following Emerald out of the parking lot and toward the Pine State Bar and Grill.

∼

"SHE REALLY IS SOMETHING," Em said, as we lurked in a booth on the restaurant side. One of the waitresses went to high school with me, and we still hung out sometimes, so I'd asked her for a table with a good view of the bar. It was late afternoon, so the place was quiet for now, everyone prepping for the dinner rush. Em and I had just eaten, but both of us would have felt like jerks if we took up a table and didn't order anything, so we both got drinks and a plate of potato skins to share.

Em and I sat on the same side of the booth, as if we were a couple. She was a lesbian and I was pansexual, so us being together wouldn't be out of the question, but we were friends. Friends plotting to take down a man.

"I'm trying to remember seeing her with anyone, and I can't. Can you?" Em asked as I shoved potato skins in my mouth out of anxiety, sour cream and cheese dripping down my chin. I was completely on board with this seduction plan, but I needed some more time to really figure it out. Plus, I didn't want Esme to see me just, like, staring at her like a creep. Like Wyatt did.

"I feel like she doesn't date a lot? But I know I've seen her with people before in a date-like context. And I went to a party once where she was with, who was that?" I had to dig back in my brain and then I snapped my greasy fingers. "Sean Corey. That's who it was. Ugh." I shuddered.

"What's wrong with Sean?"

Outwardly, nothing. Sean was a nice guy. Graduated high school and immediately went to work for his dad's landscaping business and had added caretaking to the company as well for people who only came to Maine in the summers. Sean would take care of their cottages and homes, making sure the pipes didn't freeze, the lawns got mowed, and they didn't get broken into by bored teenagers looking for something to vandalize or a place to hook up.

"Do you remember me telling you about the kid I saw eat a bunch of gum off the bottom of a bench at the planetarium?" I shuddered at the memory. I think I'd been the only one to see it, but that moment burned itself into my memory.

"Didn't that happen when you were in first grade? I'm sure he doesn't do that now," Em said, wiping her hands on a napkin. We'd demolished the potato skins, and now I was sad they were gone.

"You never know," I said in an ominous tone. A laugh snapped my attention back toward the bar. Esme popped the top of a beer and handed it to a grizzled fisherman sitting on one of the stools as if he lived there. Knowing him, he probably did. The guy was a regular.

She flipped her long dark hair over her shoulder. As long as I'd known her, Esme had always had dark hair all the way down her back that was so smooth and shiny, I'd never seen anything like it. I didn't know if I'd ever seen her with her hair completely up before.

The fisherman made another joke and she leaned her head back in laughter. Her dark eyes sparkled as she moved to the other end to tend to another customer. I couldn't stop watching the way she moved, the way she listened intently, the way she smiled.

"She really is beautiful," I said with a sigh.

"She is. So, what is the plan?" I tore my eyes away from Esme to look at Em.

"I mean, I don't know? Ordering a drink and talking to her and then asking her out seems like the way to go?" I wasn't used to being the aggressor when it came to dating. Most of the time I'd either wait to be approached, or just carry on a long-term crush without actually doing anything. It was shocking that I managed to have multiple relationships at all.

"No," Em said, waving her hand as if to erase what I'd just said. "That's no good."

I sat up, offended. "What's wrong with that plan?"

"You're not going to seduce Esme Bell by being like every other person who wants to bang her. You have to be different. You have to capture her attention. You have to be better than Wyatt. Be better than Wyatt."

Right. Wyatt. He'd asked me out in this very restaurant. I'd been on a work deadline, and it was one of the only places I would work with free internet and unlimited coffee, so I'd parked myself at the very end of the bar, and put my head-phones in. Somehow, he'd charmed me with his smile and a bad joke, and I'd shut my computer and gone to his place with him. I'd had to ask for a work extension, but the sex had been worth it. I'd expected it just to be a hookup, but then he wanted to see me again, and that was it.

In hindsight, he hadn't even had to try very hard. I wasn't sure what that said about me.

"Okay, how do I be better than Wyatt? And who made you the dating Yoda?"

Em leaned back in the booth. "I'm not saying I'm the dating Yoda. What I *am* saying is that I can offer you advice because I know you, I definitely know Wyatt, and I know enough about her to know what's going to work and what doesn't."

Plus, she'd gotten back at an ex before.

"Lay it on me," I said.

"First off, you've got to play it cool. Make her come to you. Be mysterious. Leave her wanting more." Those all sounded like tips she'd gotten from one of the terrible articles I'd had to write for a copywriting client.

"Why does this sound familiar?" I asked, and Em smirked as she showed me her phone.

"Because you literally wrote it."

Oh. It *was* one of my articles. I'd completely forgotten about writing it, which was something that happened to me a lot. The minute I was done with a project, it was like it had never existed.

"Okay, well, let me read the tips I wrote." Em handed me the phone and I scrolled through.

"Wow, this isn't that bad."

"You're such a dork sometimes," Em said, laughing.

I finished the article and then sent it to myself to digest later. "Okay, so what you're saying is that I should just dress in a sexy outfit, but not like I'm trying too hard, show up at the bar, order a drink, and then be mysterious. I can do that." I could probably do that. I hoped.

"Say something mysterious," Em prompted.

I picked up my water glass to really get into character.

"So, do you work here often?" I wiggled my eyebrows and Em groaned.

"You're just fucking with me, be serious. You have to practice so you don't do that thing where you just blank out and forget what to say."

I put my glass down. "I don't do that."

That earned me a look. "Paige. Let's be honest with ourselves about our strengths and weaknesses." Em had been reading a lot of personal development books and absorbing the information and it was starting to get on my nerves, but I kept my mouth shut. She was just trying to help.

"Fine. Okay." I picked up the glass again and tried to think of something witty that would also be mysterious. "Did you know that Cap 'n Crunch's full name is Horatio Magellan Crunch?"

Em snorted and burst out laughing. "You cannot use that as your pickup line, Paige!"

"Why not? It's cute, and informative. And it will make her wonder what else I know as far as random facts, so there's your mystery." I sat back in the booth and crossed my arms.

Em groaned. "That's enough for today. I need to get back home and let the dog out."

I picked up the tab and gave Esme one last look as she said hello to her fellow night bartender, a guy whom everyone knew as Batman, that drove an electric purple minivan and had a Great Dane named Baby that came nearly everywhere with him. In fact, Em and I went and petted Baby through the rolled-down window in his van before saying goodbye to each other and going to our respective vehicles.

"Mysterious!" Em yelled at me before she got in. "Work on it."

I PULLED into my gravel driveway and sat for a moment looking at my sweet little blue and white cottage. Sure, the paint was peeling on the shutters, and the porch dipped in some places, and the hot water wasn't always reliable, but it was mine, and I could afford the rent on it. The place belonged to an older lady who now lived full-time in Florida, and she was sweet as pie and adored me. Plus, the view was to die for.

"Hey, Potato," I called, when I walked in the door. There was no need to lock it in a town like Castleton. A large orange cat lumbered to the front door as I set down my bag and keys and meowed loudly up at me.

"Did you have fun while I was gone, sweet boy?" I rubbed the spot between his eyes that he loved and he purred so loud you could have heard him down the street. At least I had someone who was happy to see me when I got home. There were also the goldfish, Basil, Cilantro, Cumin, Paprika, and Parsley. Potato got fed first, then the fishies, who wiggled and stared at me as I watched them scoot around their tank.

"You're just so chubby and cute," I said, making fish faces at them. They didn't respond.

Potato rubbed against my legs as I heated some water in the kettle Mom had gotten me when I'd first moved in three years ago. She'd actually been a huge help with decorating and was always finding me little tchotchkes at yard sales and other places.

Since the evening was warm, I took my tea to the little screened-in porch on the back of the cottage that faced the water. Frogs sang in the pond and crickets joined them in symphony. Just feet from the end of the porch, the yard sloped and changed into a rocky shore where the water lapped restlessly. More often than not, I kept my windows open, even when it was cold, to be lulled to sleep by the sound.

Potato jumped up beside me on the wicker couch and sniffed at my cup.

"You don't want that, trust me bud," I said, moving it away from him. He gave me a glare of betrayal.

"Calm down and go find one of your fake mice to harass."

I had planning to do.

Potato jumped off the couch in a huff as I pulled up my social media accounts. I was lucky that in a small town, everyone just followed everyone without thinking too much about it. Made it a lot easier to see what Esme was up to. Fuck, she really was gorgeous. Just... wow.

I scrolled through shot after shot of her mashed into groups of smiling people, including patrons from the bar. There were plenty of solo pics as well, showcasing her sleeve of artistic wildflower tattoos, legs for days, and the most perfectly shaped ass I'd ever seen.

There were also some posts about her dog, a husky named Stormy, and one or two with her dad, Butch.

My deep dive went way too deep and my finger slipped and I ended up liking one of her posts from like three years ago. I undid it a second later, but my heart would not stop slamming itself against my chest.

"That's enough stalking for today," I said, closing the app and turning on some music instead. Time for more tea. And plotting. I still thought my cereal fact opener was a winner, and I was going to prove Em wrong.

It was on.

Chapter Two

"AND YOU WON'T BELIEVE it, the starter kit is only ninety-nine dollars!" my mom said, when I stopped at her house in the morning before heading to work at the local café. Her eyes were frenzied and bright behind her reading glasses, which hung on a chain so she didn't lose them. I'd gotten her this particular pair for her birthday last year.

I rubbed my forehead. "Mom, we've been through this before. Do I need to show you the FTC website again?"

I loved her, but she fell for scams as easily as I fell for hot people that hated commitment.

"Don't you want to support me?" she said with a pout. *Here we go again.*

"Yes, but not like this." We sat down to the table as she set a plate of biscuits and gravy and a bowl of fruit in front of me. There was also fresh coffee with my favorite caramel creamer steaming in a pottery mug. If I had to suffer through another one of her sales pitches, at least I had a delicious breakfast to get me through it. One thing I could say for my mom: she could cook. I'd grown up completely spoiled in the food department. I was the only kid who'd brought three flavors of macarons to the bake sale.

"I really think you could be good at it. You have too many jobs," she said.

"Right, and I don't need another one," I said.

Temporarily defeated, she pursed her lips and sat down with me. From experience, I knew that she was only taking a break. She'd be back to trying to win me over in no time. I'd played this game too many times before.

She sipped her coffee and hummed to herself for a few minutes while I waited for the other shoe to drop.

Mom inhaled through her nose and spoke. "Do you think Wyatt could come over and take a look at the sink?" Hello, second shoe. I stifled a groan of irritation.

I set my fork down so I didn't throw it across the room. "Mom, you know we're not together. He doesn't have to come fix things anymore. If you want him to fix things, then *you* date him." She choked on a sip of coffee.

"Paige, that's ridiculous," she said, one hand fluttering in the air as if brushing away the suggestion.

No, what was ridiculous was sometimes I thought my mom had liked Wyatt more than she liked me. I mean, there was a reason I'd thrown all my sense out the window and fallen for him. Wyatt Witmer was a charmer, through and through. He'd completely won her over and sometimes I would come over to visit her and find him hanging a picture or messing with her TV or doing some other house thing that my mom apparently needed a man to do, and my heart would melt all over again and all the red flags would get shoved to the back closet of my mind again.

My dad had left when I was a toddler and Mom never really settled into doing things on her own. I had wished and wished that she would find someone to take care of her, but that person never materialized, so I took up the mantle as best I could.

Sure, I couldn't keep her from getting sucked into marketing scams, or fix her leaky sink, but I knew how to call a repairman and help her organize her taxes, and make sure the mortgage was paid. I did the best that I could, and I always would. When Wyatt was around, it had been nice to have someone else help out.

"I can call someone to fix the sink," I said, getting up to take my empty plate and bowl to the sink. I really needed to get to work. My to-do list was longer than a CVS receipt.

"No, no, it's fine," she said, blowing me off and finishing her coffee. She always did that. Acted like things were no big deal and then was astonished when stuff inevitably broke.

I kissed her on the cheek as I gathered up my stuff. "I love you, I'll let you know about the sink." Time to make my escape.

"Okay, think about the business opportunity!" she called as I walked through the door and shut it behind me. I didn't respond.

I WAS SO full from breakfast that I didn't feel like eating again until the early afternoon, so I packed up my laptop and stuff from the café, and headed to Sweet's Sweets, the local bakery my best friend Linley Sweet's family owned.

"Hey, Martha," I said to her mom, who was behind the counter. "Is she in the back?"

Martha beamed at me, and it was like looking at Linley in the future. That apple fell directly from that tree. "Hey Paige, go on back. She'll be glad to see you." I pushed through the Employees ONLY door and found Linley humming as she rolled out a massive rectangle of dough on the long stainless counter that took up most of the middle of the room.

"Hey, whatcha making?" I said and she jumped as she looked up. She had flour on her glasses, but that was nothing new.

"Hey, Paige. What's up?"

I pulled up a stool and watched as she finished rolling out the dough that turned out to be for cinnamon rolls, but these were no ordinary cinnamon rolls. Sweet's always did seasonal cinnamon rolls and these were the summer peach rolls, with fresh peaches, peach jam, and a cream cheese frosting. Later in the summer they'd switch to wild Maine blueberry, which was always my favorite.

"I'm going to destroy my ex," I said, watching her spreading out a huge bowl of freshly sliced peaches on the dough. She paused, peaches dripping from her hand.

"Okay? Explain."

I laid out the plan while she finished filing the dough. Watching her roll it up was literally my favorite part, so I was glad I'd gotten here when I did.

Martha came back to see how everything was going, and to ask if Linley was going to have time to work on a wedding cake. Her dad, Mitch, lumbered through with a massive bag of flour over his shoulder and grunted at me. He didn't speak much but made the best bagels in the entire world.

Once she'd dealt with her parents, Linley turned her attention back to me as she washed her hands. She pulled a container down from a shelf and shoved it toward me. She always saved a few extras for me when I came over. I had to convince her constantly that I was friends with her not just because she gave me free delicious treats.

"All I can think about are all the ways this isn't going to work out the way you think it's going to work out. What if she just turns you down?" she asked.

I opened the container to find lemon sandwich cookies. They were so sweet and tart they were going to make my teeth hurt, but I didn't even care.

"Are you doubting my powers of seduction?" I said, before sinking my teeth into one of the cookies. Perfection. I licked the powdered sugar from my lips.

"No, but if she doesn't want to date you, then this whole thing is going to fall apart."

"I'm not going to *date* her, I'm just going to *bang* her and gloat about it."

Linley gave me a look as she started the rolling process. "I mean, do what you want, but I don't have a whole lot of confidence in this master plan."

I narrowed my eyes. "You're supposed to support me. You're my best friend."

"I don't have to support you when you're doing something ridiculous."

She picked up the sharpest knife in the kitchen that would cut through the dough without crushing it. I'd seen her do this complete process so many times. She'd never once let me help, and I'd stopped asking many years ago. It made sense. I'd probably come up with some shitty looking rolls that they wouldn't be able to sell.

"You supported me when I tried to do my own mermaid hair," I pointed out.

Linley let the knife slide through the dough and then turned the newly formed roll onto its side and set it on the baking sheet.

"And how did that turn out? Your tub is still purple."

I snatched a second cookie from the tub. "That's not the point."

She pressed her lips together and didn't say anything else, which I guess was her way of supporting me. I'd take it.

Martha bustled back and handed me a box. "I made you a sandwich and threw a few other little things in there."

"Thanks, Martha," I said, taking the bag. Linley looked up when her mom didn't immediately leave the kitchen and continued to hover.

"So, you up to anything this weekend? Going out?" Her eyes went from me to Linley and back.

When Linley didn't answer, I did. "Maybe. We hadn't talked about it yet."

"Well, you should. It's good for you to go out." This comment was directed at Linley. It was her mother's fondest wish for her to find someone to marry, or at least be with for the long-term. She was also desperate for grandchildren, but one step at a time.

I watched Linley's jaw clench. Honestly, her mom was being sweet, but I could see it from Linley's side as well. At least her mom wasn't pushing her to get back with her shitty ex like mine had done for weeks after my breakup.

When neither of us said anything else, Martha left and Linley sighed the longest sigh.

"She's really ramped up the relationship pressure, huh?" I questioned. Linley started cutting the cinnamon rolls a little more viciously.

"I get it," she said, arranging the rolls on the tray so she could let them rise a second time. "She doesn't want me to be alone, but I'm just like, I can't have a relationship very easily when I'm up at 4 am making bread nearly every morning. I'm fucking tired." She slammed her hands down on the counter. "I'm so fucking tired."

I could tell. Even her voice was weary. I hopped off my stool and put my arms around her.

"Hey, it's okay. You deserve more time off. Do you want to come over tonight and I'll make you dinner? Or I can bring dinner to your place." She'd recently gotten her own apartment in the swanky new building in town. Her mom hadn't taken the move well, and I think that was what was responsible for most of the increased helicopter parenting activity.

Linley gave me a weak smile. "Dinner that I don't have to make sounds great."

"I'll bring it to you," I said. "Wear your onesie and I'll be there at seven."

She gave me a thumbs up and went back to slicing. Figuring I should probably get out of her hair, I gave her another hug and grabbed my treats and waved goodbye to Martha.

Maybe once I'd gotten my revenge on Wyatt, I could put my energy into finding someone decent for Linley. She deserved someone great. But first, I was going to make my ex suffer.

I STOPPED at the organic grocery store that Esme's father owned to get a few ingredients to make Linley dinner. She loved my chicken pot pie soup, so that was on the menu.

"Making something special tonight?" Butch asked as he slid the items through the scanner and tossed them toward the teen bagger, who looked like she'd rather be doing anything else.

Part of getting groceries here was having a chat with Butch. That man got all of his energy out of a good gab session.

"Just a chicken pot pie soup," I said. He nodded and finished scanning as I slid my credit card into the slot.

"Sounds great. You should submit the recipe on our website. You could win a free gift card!" I nodded and he continued to talk about a chicken soup he made, listing the ingredients, and how to make it, even though I hadn't asked any questions about it.

Finally, I had my groceries and I could leave. I gave him a

smile and realized how much he looked like his daughter. I stumbled and nearly dropped all my bags before regaining my footing and walking out to my car.

"THAT WAS AMAZING," Linley said, folding both hands on her stomach. Instead of sitting at her little dining table, we'd taken to the couch, and I was in my comfiest sweat suit while she rocked a onesie with a unicorn horn on the hood. We were both peak cozy.

"I didn't do too bad this time." I set my empty bowl on the coffee table and kicked my feet up.

"Seriously, thank you." Linley took the dishes to the sink and pulled some ice cream out of the freezer. Instead of using bowls, we just stuck our spoons in the caramel and pretzel swirl ice cream.

"Anytime, friend." I stabbed my spoon into the ice cream and then shoved it in my mouth.

"So, what is this grand plan with Esme?" she asked. I'd just hit a river of caramel and was doing my best to get as much of it on my spoon as possible.

"Dazzling her with my wits, taking her back to my cottage, showing her my cat, and then sleeping with her. And then rubbing it in Wyatt's face." It was pretty simple.

"Showing her your cat? Is that a new thing I don't know about?"

I blinked at her for a second. "No, I'm literally going to show her Potato."

"What if she's allergic to cats?"

"She's not allergic to cats." I pushed her spoon away and we fought for a second with the ice cream.

"How do you know?" She pointed at me with her spoon.

I had to think about that. "Okay, so maybe I'm not positive

about that, but it doesn't matter. If all else fails, I'll show her my tits." They were pretty great.

Linley rolled her eyes. "She works in a bar. I'm sure she sees tits every shift."

"You know you're really killing my ice cream buzz," I said.

"Sorry. I'll stop."

There was a moment of silence as we each tried to think of how to change the subject.

"Do you want to go out this weekend? I'm happy to, even to just get your mom off your back. I could grab Em, I know she'd want to come."

"Why not?" Linley said, scraping the bottom of the ice cream tub. I was completely and totally full and not ready to move yet.

"Cool. We could go out, out. Like, out of town. So we don't see people from Castleton."

"Wait, there are people who don't live in Castleton?" Linley gasped dramatically.

"I know, right? Imagine."

We both laughed and then talked about where we should go and what we should do.

"As long as I don't have to dance," she said. "I don't dance."

"Wait, you don't? This is brand new information."

She rolled her eyes. "Yes, I know, but you're one of the few people who have seen me dance."

I cringed at the memory.

"Exactly," she said.

"Your mom really did you a disservice not putting you in dance class when you were a kid."

"Oh no, she did. I got kicked out."

That was news to me.

"They kicked you out of dance class? Why?"

Linley grinned. "I may have bit one of the other dancers."

I put my hand up. "I'm sorry, you bit one of the other kids?"

"To be fair, we were five years old, and she was mean as hell."

I didn't know how to respond to that. "Wait, did you bite someone I'd know?"

"Angie Moore."

The mention of her name made me automatically recoil. "Yeah, you were right to bite her. She's a bitch."

I'd had an altercation with her at camp one summer that I still didn't talk about with anyone, not even my mom.

"Exactly. She had it coming."

Linley and I talked about our disdain for Angie until Linley started yawning and I knew she had to get to bed. Having a friend that woke up before the sun was weird as hell when I was used to pulling all-nighters to meet deadlines.

"Someday we'll have jobs with normal hours," I said. "That's the dream."

She yawned again and gave me a limp hug. "Go to bed," I said, and let myself out of her house. No doubt she'd end up passed out on the couch. Been there, done that.

Potato was grumpy when I got back and screamed at me the whole time I was in the shower. To appease him, and to make him stop, I gave him a few spoonfuls of tuna.

"You are literally the most spoiled cat I've ever seen. You're lucky you got me as your mom." He just rubbed his face on mine and I tried not to recoil from his tuna breath.

Work was calling, but I knew if I started anything, I wouldn't be able to stop, and I had to set better boundaries. Or at least start thinking about setting better boundaries. Something something balance.

Instead, I tried to find out if Esme Bell was allergic to cats via her social media posts.

Chapter Three

I DIDN'T GET ANYWHERE with finding out about Esme's cat opinions, but I did get to see her gorgeous face a bunch, so that wasn't completely wasted time.

I had a full inbox of new assignments, deadlines, and requests for changes when I looked at my phone the next morning. A headache was already starting to camp out behind my eyes.

"Remind me not to read work emails in bed," I said to a sleeping Potato before hauling myself out of bed and going to the kitchen for my first caffeine infusion of the day.

While I had my coffee and then microwaved a frozen egg sandwich to get something in my stomach, I flagged my messages for priority and scheduled my day. There was no way I could keep track of everything without lots and lots of charts and calendars. I had content and copywriting gigs, editing jobs, captioning work, and I also did some social media management as well. When it came to work, I got bored easily, and I didn't like to put all my eggs in one basket, so now I was just juggling a ton of baskets and trying not to drop them and break too many eggs.

~

THE CASTLETON CAFÉ was packed when I slid into a corner next to one of the many outlets. I set my water bottle next to my laptop to remind myself to hydrate and started the first thing on my list: a complete rewrite of an article that I'd busted my ass to get finished before a ridiculous deadline, which apparently was the opposite of what the company actually wanted. Go figure. Rewriting it in the style they wanted, along with fitting in the right SEO terms and affiliate links, took me through my second cup of coffee.

By the time I was midway editing another article for an online beauty blog, I needed something else to eat, so I waited in line for a small salad, trying not to be bitter about all the tourists hanging around. Sure, I liked being in a busy café because it was much nicer than being alone, but I hated having to wait in line behind people who had apparently never ordered a coffee before and didn't know how.

At last, it was my turn. "Hey, Tabitha, can I get a chicken César and a lemonade?" I asked. Tabitha had been the secretary of my elementary school but had retired to run the café when it had gone up for sale a few years ago.

"Sure, hon," she said, tapping the order into the computer. A crash from the back room made us both flinch.

"Jesus, Sonny, be careful!" she yelled over her shoulder. Her son, the guy named Sonny, poked his head out with a goofy smile. I couldn't believe he was a whole grown human. I'd babysat him what felt like yesterday and now he was old enough to have a job and facial hair.

He tossed his hair out of his face. "Sorry! Nothing's broken."

Tabitha's eyes narrowed. "That means something is definitely broken. Blue, take over." Blue, nicknamed for their bright hair and electric blue wheelchair, rolled in as Tabitha went to see what chaos Sonny was causing.

"I'll get that right out for you," Blue said, grabbing a cup and going to fix my drink. I went back to my table and waited. Tabitha was giving Sonny a piece of her mind, and I pretended not to try and eavesdrop. A couple at the next table over was in from out of town and were clearly not having a good time, so my attention was torn. This was why I had to put on my headphones and a podcast on most days. People around me were just too interesting. My productivity went dramatically down in the summer when everyone was here.

Blue rolled over with my drink and salad on a little tray and I took it from them.

"Thanks so much," I said. "I'll probably need more caffeine as soon as I'm done with this."

"Hey, as long as you're not ordering a semi-dry cappuccino and then bitching when it isn't dry enough for you, we're good." Blue gave me a wink and went back behind the counter.

"What the hell even is a dry cappuccino?" I said to myself, and then looked it up on the internet because I just had to know.

THIRTY MINUTES later I was reading about Ethiopian coffee beans and I'd ignored five emails that had just come in. Oops.

A notification came in from my freelancer group chat. The current topic of conversation was helping Ash with an email to a client that was refusing to pay her. I didn't have anything to add, so I just scrolled through the other messages. Jen was still dealing with her recent breakup, and CJ was asking for advice on plants for their new apartment. There were also three other people: Lin, Faith, and Rya. We'd all sort of found each other online and through different jobs and decided we needed a support group for ourselves. Freelancing could be lonely as hell.

Already distracted, I also checked in on the auction for a vintage jigsaw puzzle that was a cover of one of the most-famous romance authors, Barbara Cartland. My bid was still winning, but there was more than a week left, so things could still turn, but I really wanted to add it to my vintage puzzle collection. Unlike a lot of people, I actually put mine together. With gloves, of course.

I rounded out my afternoon captioning a video for an influencer, which was one of my most-enjoyable jobs. I'd taken a training course on a whim and found out that I was both good at it and I enjoyed doing it. I worked for one company, and I also sought out other jobs and had a steady roster of people that needed me.

My brain reached its limit and I had to take a break and shut the computer to give my eyes a rest. Sure, I had blue-light glasses, but they could only do so much. I packed up my stuff and took it to my car. I'd been sitting so long, my body was stiff, so I decided to take a walk around the tiny downtown area. I really needed to add regular exercise into my day.

Castleton boasted one lighthouse, two beaches, three restaurants, one bar, one bakery, a post office, an insurance company, a real estate office, a café, and a bookstore that was attached to the tiny library. Sure, it wasn't a big town, but we even had a little movie theater that had a stage for the community theater productions and local orchestra concerts.

When the wind blew just right, you could smell the ocean, and if you walked all the way to the edge of the main parking lot behind the main strip of businesses, you could see the water and the small dock that people used to take their boats out.

On a whim, I walked toward the dock and slipped my

shoes off and dipped my toes in the water. Even though it was the height of summer, the ocean never got that warm. You had to be a hearty soul to go swimming in the ocean in Maine, but I did as much as I could, all year round. I liked the shock of cold. It energized me. Everyone I knew said I was a weirdo.

I took a quick little video swishing my feet and posted it on my social. A few "likes" came in and there was one I didn't expect: esmeybe. I checked to make sure that was still Esme's account. It was. Maybe she clicked by mistake? Nope, several minutes later, the like was still there.

Thinking about her looking at my social media made my insides squirm. Not that I didn't know she was following me, but it was different now. Knowing that she saw all the silly stuff I put on my pages made me wonder what she thought about me.

Linley was probably right. This plan was doomed to failure.

And then I got a text from Wyatt that was just a picture of his penis, followed by a hasty **sorry that was for someone else** and I decided the plan was back on.

"SO, when are you actually going to approach her? Or are you going to spend the rest of the summer just... lurking?" Linley said that Friday night as we sat in the Pine State Bar and Grill and I kept one eye on the bar as I scanned my menu. During the tourist season, it changed weekly with what was available, so there was always something new to try.

"I'm working on it, okay?" I said.

Our waitress, Dawn, whose daughter Amanda I had hooked up with in high school in a frenzy of I don't know what during the Fourth of July, came over to take our orders. I blushed whenever I saw her because she and Amanda had the same eyes and smile. Amanda had run off to fashion school in New York and had kissed this town goodbye. She was apparently dating an up-and-coming actress who'd just landed a starring role in a show, so I'd probably never see her again. Missed opportunity right there.

"I'll have the summer shrimp salad," I mumbled, and Linley got the same.

I was about to ask her where she wanted to go after this (we still hadn't come up with a concrete plan other than "going out to appease her mother"), when she gasped.

"Oh my god, don't look now, but Wyatt is here."

I couldn't escape that fucker, I swear.

"Seriously?" I said under my breath, keeping my head down. If there was enough room, I would have crawled under the table.

"Yeah, and I have some bad news. He's with Gretchen Johnson," she said.

My stomach dropped into my shoes.

"Of course he fucking is."

It was totally normal that he had moved on from me to the girl who had once shoved a used tampon in my locker in high school and made my life a living hell, but never got caught because her dad was a county sheriff and everyone was scared of him.

"What are they doing?" I asked. Linley looked around me to the front entrance.

"Keep your head down," she hissed, trying to shield me with the dessert menu. I froze as I heard Wyatt's voice and then Gretchen's laugh. Heinous bitch.

They walked right by me, so close I could smell Wyatt's deodorant. He'd never worn cologne, or any other scent, and I'd always liked the way he smelled. Wyatt and Gretchen seemed completely wrapped up in each other as they took a high-top for two in the bar area and she draped herself all over him.

"Do you want to leave?" Linley asked. "I'm absolutely fine with going somewhere else. We could even get the salads to go and eat them at my place."

I shook my head. "No, I'm not letting him drive me out. If everyone in this town had to avoid their exes, there would be no one left."

Linley snorted. "True enough."

All I had to do was avoid drawing his attention or having him look over at me for any reason. Easy.

"Do you want to switch places?" Linley asked.

Just as I was about to say yes, Wyatt zoned in on me while Gretchen was checking something on her phone. He gave me a little nod of recognition and then a rakish wink.

I gave him one of my fingers in the air and he just laughed. Gretchen said something to him and he shook his head.

"I'm going to murder him," I said. My hands shook with how mad I was.

"No murdering," Linley said, taking my hands and squeezing them. "Let's go, come on."

"No. I'm not leaving."

Instead, we switched places so that I wouldn't have to see his annoying face.

Dawn brought our salads, but even food couldn't distract me from whatever he was doing with Gretchen. It was like he'd planned this, even though it was impossible for him to know that I'd be here with Linley. Nearly everyone local here knew that he and I had dated, and that he'd dumped me.

No doubt people were talking about how he was moving on with someone new, which meant they were talking about how I wasn't.

I hated it here sometimes.

"Excuse me," a voice said behind my shoulder. Linley looked up and then her fork clattered on her plate.

Slowly, I swiveled around and found myself looking up at Esme, who had a drink in one hand. What the hell was happening.

She tossed her hair over her shoulder and leaned down so no one would overhear her. "Hey, sorry to bother you, but Wyatt sent this over. I can absolutely take it back if you don't want it. I know what he did to you." Her bartender smile slipped for a moment. I could barely breathe as I stared at lips that glistened with a dark lipstick in the light of the fake candles on the table.

"He asked me to just send you a Jaeger bomb, but I made something a little more special. It's called a paloma. Seemed more your speed." She set the slightly pink drink down in front of me.

"Thank you," I finally said, after looking back and forth at the drink and at Linley, who was similarly stunned. Esme stood up and gave me a wink before doing a little spin.

"Let me know how you like it," she said over her shoulder.

I gaped as she walked back to the bar, her heels making an audible click on the floor, even through the rest of the noise around us.

"Help," I said, after I finally tore my eyes away from her.

"I don't even like women, but holy shit. If she formed a cult, I would join it," Linley said, her face a little red.

"Can you believe Wyatt had the gall to send this over?" I said, pointing to it. Esme hadn't said what was in it, but I was going to drink it anyway. "What if Wyatt didn't really send it? What if she's just *pretending* he did so she could come over and talk to me?" I should have said more to her. I should have flirted, but I'd been so caught off guard.

Linley glanced over my shoulder once and then back at me.

"I don't think so. Wyatt just mouthed 'you're welcome' at me. So I'm guessing he did send it. Fucker."

I sighed. "This is a conundrum. On one hand, Wyatt is involved in the existence of this drink. On the other, Esme made it for me, and I need to get in good with her. Fuck it." I picked up the drink and stood up, turning to the side so Wyatt would be sure to see me, but not facing him directly.

My plan to chug the drink was hampered by the amount of ice in the glass, so I succeeded at dumping a lot of it on myself, but whatever. The point was made. I slammed the glass on the table and then sat down.

"You have a little something," Linley said, waving to her chest area.

"Yes, I'm aware. It didn't go as smoothly as I planned." I wiped myself off as best I could.

"Was it good, at least?"

"Yeah, tasted like grapefruit." I licked my lips and grinned. "I feel like I should have another one."

Linley sniffed the empty glass. "I feel like you shouldn't do that, because you're my ride."

Good point.

"Fine, but I'm definitely getting one of those again sometime."

Linley looked at her phone. "If we want to get anywhere, we should head out now. Let's go, Designated Driver." She made a sound like the crack of a whip.

I grumbled, but she was picking up the tab for tonight. I was more than happy to take one for the team in service of Linley having a night out where she didn't have to bake anything.

WE ENDED up at an Irish pub about an hour away from Castleton. It was Linley's idea.

"We're here for the culture," she yelled over the speakers blasting Dropkick Murphys. Classic.

"Right," I said, as she sipped her beer and looked around. I'd just gotten a soda, but we'd ordered a basket of hot wings and fries. This wasn't just a night out. I was on a mission to get my friend a man. Or at least a number so she could get her mom off her back for a little while.

"There are just so many dudes in here," I said, leaning close to her. There was some sort of sporting event blasting on the massive TV screens. I couldn't get distracted. It was time to focus.

"Is there something wrong with that?" Linley asked. "My mom would be thrilled."

We both laughed about that.

"I wonder if you can order a husband?" I asked, looking at the menu.

Linley picked up the menu and pretended to scan it. "Nothing. Damn."

Even though I wasn't drunk, or even tipsy, being with someone who was getting there was giving me a pleasant contact buzz.

I snuck a sip of her beer as she scanned the room. "I should probably talk with at least one guy tonight, so I can tell my mom."

Her mom would spot a lie a mile away, so there was no use trying to pull one over on her. We'd tried and failed.

"Okay, avoid that one," I said, pointing to one guy laughing robustly at the bar.

"Why?"

"Because he looks like someone who would have sexually harassed me in high school." It wasn't anything specific about the guy. It was an energy he gave off. A vibe.

Linley tilted her head to the side, considering. "I think you're projecting."

I didn't think I was.

She took another sip of her beer. "Still, he's not my type anyway. I don't like blond guys for some reason. They don't seem very trustworthy."

"Now who's projecting?" I asked, reaching for another wing.

"I can't help what my heart wants," she said.

I completely got what she was saying. Wyatt had blond hair. Hmmm.

Knowing what I did about Linley's preferences, I took a visual sweep around the room. We had very different types. She was into much more sporty guys than I was. Wyatt had been an exception for me, and one upside of not dating him anymore was that I didn't have to hear about his gym workouts anymore. At the time, I'd forced myself to listen to "be supportive" while I'd been dying on the inside. I really was an excellent girlfriend.

"There," I said, leaning toward her. "Two tables over. He's alone."

Linley pretended to gaze around at the bar so she could get a good look at the guy I'd spotted. He wasn't exactly sporty per-se, but there was something about him that I thought she might like.

Linley gave him a long appraisal. "Oh, yeah. He *is* cute."

I shoved her with my shoulder. "Go talk to him. If he's a cool guy, he'll think it's hot that you approached him. If not, then you know he's not for you."

Linley's face got a little red, but she hopped off her seat and squared her shoulders before stepping in the direction of the potential suitor.

I couldn't hear what she said to him, but he gave her a little smile and she slid into the empty seat next to him. My work here was done.

To avoid being a complete helicopter friend, I pulled out

my phone to give myself something to do while Linley worked her magic. She was the kind of person who was so warm, she could have a chat with anybody and make them feel like she was completely invested. Sometimes that backfired and she neglected her own needs and wants to cater to other people. That had been an issue in some of her past relationships, in my opinion.

I zipped through my notifications and shuddered at the memory of Wyatt's dick pic. Not because he had a bad dick (he didn't. It was very nice), but because it meant he was sending them to other people. He'd probably been doing that while we were dating. I'd heard rumors but had ignored them at the time. I'd believed Wyatt when he explained everything away. Fuck, I'd been so consumed with lust that I'd ignored all sense. More brain, less horny next time.

I hadn't been looking through my phone for long when Linley came back with a grin on her face. "He had to go, but I got his number and he followed me on social, so who knows?"

I gave her my full attention. "Details?"

"His name is Gray, he only lives about a half hour from Castleton, twenty-six, and he's a phlebotomist."

"I have no idea what that means."

"He draws blood. He made a cute little vampire joke, so I'm thinking I should definitely go out with him."

She wouldn't stop grinning and going on about him, so I was thrilled for her. Linley downed the rest of her beer and I asked if she was ready to go out on a high note.

"Yeah, I'm good." Since she was used to getting up so early, she went to bed much earlier than I did.

Linley paid the tab in exchange for me driving and we headed out.

I put my arm around her shoulders as we walked back to where my car was parked. The night air was thick and warm, and I couldn't wait to get back to my sweet little cottage and the cool seaside air. "So, that wasn't so bad, was it? Going out. Your mom was right."

Linley groaned. "She's going to be insufferable for a month at least."

"Is that better than her nagging you?"

We reached my car and I unlocked the door so she could slide in. "I'll let you know."

Chapter Four

ANOTHER WEEK, another to-do list. I was back at the café tweaking a draft of an article when I happened to look up and see who was next in line to order.

"Iced dirty marshmallow chai with three shots of espresso, please," Esme said. Tabitha was running things while Blue was on their break. Sonny puttered around clearing up the dishes with earbuds blasting something extremely loud.

It was weird seeing Esme outside of the restaurant context. Sure, I did see her other places, but not very often. I got the feeling she worked a lot of hours.

"Sure thing, hon," Tabitha said, snapping her fingers at Sonny to wipe down a table in the back.

Esme leaned against the counter. "Oh, and one of the cherry turnovers, if you have any left."

I watched her over the top of my laptop. Her gauzy sundress swirled when the door opened and someone new walked in. Not something she'd wear at the bar, that was for sure. It was her signature black, though. The only other color I'd seen her in was dark purple.

So entranced with watching Esme wait for her order, I

didn't see when a group of tourists piled in behind her, claiming every single available table. Tabitha handed Esme her drink and turnover and suddenly there was only one seat left: At my table. I forced my face into something that I hoped looked like deep concentration as I stared at my laptop screen.

"Hey, is this seat taken?" she asked. I looked up and stopped breathing for a second. Wow. She wore dark makeup around her eyes, but it totally worked on her. I would look like a weird goth clown. She looked like a fallen angel. Ready to sin.

"No, yes, I mean, sure," I said, which didn't really answer her question. Instead I just pushed the chair out with my foot. That was a clear enough signal.

"Thanks, Paige," she said. I knew who she was. She knew who I was. Still, hearing my name come from her mouth was both startling and... kind of hot.

"You're welcome," I said. This was the second time she'd surprised me, and I wasn't dressed that cute today either. Unless you counted a tank top that referenced one of my favorite TV shows and my favorite baggy linen pants so I didn't sweat too much. The café didn't have air conditioning, so the only moving air was from fans and sometimes opening the front and back doors.

I'd picked out the outfit that I'd planned to wear to the bar when I put my seduction plan in action: A white silk top that made my chest look amazing, and a black skirt that somehow made my legs look longer than they were. Esme would have been swept off her feet by my effortless coolness. That had been the plan, but alas, the plan was in the trash now. Could I get a do-over?

Esme looked down at her turnover and then up at me. "Are you working? I don't want to distract you." Her very presence was distracting. There was no working with her sitting there, so close that our feet kept bumping into each other every time I fidgeted because she made me so nervous.

"I mean, sort of. Not really. I was just about to take a break," I lied.

Esme broke off a corner of her turnover and popped it in her mouth. Her lipstick today was so red that I couldn't stop looking at her mouth and that pop of color.

She smiled. "Look, I wanted to apologize for the whole Wyatt drink thing." I was wondering when that was going to come up.

"It's fine," I said, even though it wasn't fine.

"No, it was an asshole thing to do and he made me participate. I hope you liked the drink at least?"

I nodded, hopefully not too enthusiastically. "Yeah, it was amazing. I'd never had one before."

She tore off another bite of turnover. "I'll make you one, anytime."

"Thanks," I said.

"Want some?" she said, after a few moments of silence as I stared at her and tried to figure out what to say.

"Yeah, sure." I would have taken a piece of gum she'd pulled off the underside of the table. Our fingers brushed as she handed me a bit of the flaky turnover. Crumbs dusted my laptop, but that was why I had a cover on my keyboard.

"You off work today?" I asked, after devouring the bite and wiping my mouth and hoping I'd caught all the crumbs.

Esme sighed and sat back in her chair. "Yeah, I took a mental health day. We all need those, you know?"

I was familiar with the concept, but I rarely gave myself days off. Breaks, yes. But entire days? I needed to learn her ways.

The sound in the café grew louder as more and more people walked in.

"What the hell is going on?" I asked, looking around at the

crowd. You could barely move now, there were so many people standing around.

"It's the Summer Daze Sale," she said. Right. I'd forgotten about that. Several of the local businesses got together for a mid-summer push, which meant lots of discounts and activities in town, and tons of tourists wandering about and being generally annoying.

"These things always sneak up on me," I said, finally shutting my laptop. There was no point in keeping up appearances. To keep my fingers from trembling, I knit them together on top of the table. I'd probably just had too much caffeine.

"My dad will no doubt come home with a trunk full of shit he doesn't need because 'it was on sale!' and then I'll have to find space for it." She laughed. That sounded exactly like Butch, from what I knew about him.

"Oh, do you live together?" I hadn't known that. There was only so much you could glean from social media sometimes. Esme didn't seem to share a whole lot of her family or really personal life stuff. I'd done a deep dive trying to find her hobbies, but no luck so far, other than walking her dog.

"Yeah, it's been just the two of us my whole life. Well, and Stormy." I'd forgotten that she was also an only child.

"I know what that's like," I said through a sigh. Esme kept picking apart her turnover with surgical precision. Her nails were sharp like daggers and covered with a polish that was the color of dried blood.

She was just so damn cool.

"It was just you and your mom, right?" she asked. The world narrowed to the area of my table, and the two of us. The café noise faded away, and I got completely mesmerized by her eyes. They were a light brown near the iris, and a darker brown around the outside. I'd always loved brown eyes.

"I had to get my own place," I said, a little breathlessly. My brain snapped back into reality. What was I doing? I wasn't supposed to be gazing into her eyes. *I* was supposed to be seducing *her*.

Right, seduction.

"Out by River Road, right?" Esme said, and I sat back in shock. I didn't know she knew where I lived. To be fair, I did know where her dad, and I guess her as well, lived. I drove by it every day on my way to the café.

"That's right," I said, and then decided it was time to test the waters. "You should come over sometime. My porch is right on the water, and it's beautiful at night." There. That wasn't *too* suggestive, but it was just suggestive enough.

Esme sipped her drink through the straw and then licked her lips. I could feel the blood pounding in my ears, and my skin got tight.

"That would be great. It's nice to get out, since having a roommate who is also your dad can be a little weird sometimes," she said.

I couldn't imagine. I'd left my mom's house for college and had never looked back. Even when I had to live in the shittiest of shitty apartments with a ton of roommates, I refused to live with her again.

"Sure, yeah, you can come over anytime you want." *Whoa there, getting a little reckless, Paige. Rein it in.*

"Really? That would be great, but I'm usually working most nights. Unless you want to hang out at 2am." She let out a little laugh that made my stomach flip over.

"Okay," I blurted out. "I'm a night owl anyway." I mean, that wasn't completely true, but whatever. I'd take what I could get, even if it was at 2am.

Esme raised her eyebrows. "Are you sure?"

"Absolutely," I said, choking on my own saliva somehow. I coughed and had to wipe my face with a napkin. Smooth. Really smooth. I was an excellent seducer.

"That would be great," Esme said, with a smile that

warmed me from the inside out. She picked up her phone and asked me for my number. I listed it off for her and then she sent me a message of "hi" and a smiley face.

I wasn't sure how I'd done it, but I'd cleared the first hurdle: getting her number. I'd never had the guts to message any of her social media pages, even after she'd liked one of my posts.

Esme started to get up and I didn't know what else to do to make her stay. I did need to get some more work done, but I didn't want her to go yet.

"So, I guess I'll see you around?" she asked.

"Yup," I said. Brilliant. Amazing.

Esme gave me a little nod and then started to walk away, before spinning back around, her dress swirling perfectly, as if she was a model.

"See you later, Paige."

"You too," I blurted out.

"HOLY SHIT," I said, removing my headphones as Em took the seat that Esme had vacated a few hours ago.

"Hello, friend," she said. "You look like you're in a work daze."

"I am," I said, rubbing my eyes and taking my blue light glasses off. "What's up?"

"I figured I would come and see you in your natural habitat."

I snorted. "How was your day?"

Em made a face. She worked answering phones for her uncle's insurance company. Not the most thrilling work, but there were donuts from Sweet's and she got to wear jeans every Friday, so that was something.

"I hate it, but then I'm afraid to get something else I'd

hate more, you know? I can pretty much get away with reading smut on one screen while I manage invoices and emails on the other." A steady paycheck was almost worth it, in my opinion. I'd never really been able to stick with that kind of job. I couldn't do one thing for eight hours a day, five days a week, without feeling my entire soul dying slowly in my chest.

"Plus, I get weekends off, so I can work on my other stuff. Speaking of that, you want to come shell hunting with me this weekend?" Em collected seashells and made them into art, sometimes crushing them and making beautiful coasters with the bits mixed with resin, or she used whole shells to make wreaths or lampshades. She sold everything online and didn't make much, but that wasn't why she did it. Making things fed her soul in a way that her job never could.

"Someday, I'm going to have enough supplies for a whole coffee table," she said. One of her big goals was to collect enough beautiful shells to arrange in a mosaic between two pieces of glass. She'd been collecting for years, but still didn't have enough of the "good shells," whatever that meant.

"Yeah, that sounds great. I'll bring my suit and we can take a swim too," I said.

"Good deal. Now that's out of the way, how are you doing with ruining my brother's life?" I was glad I had some positive news to report.

"Funny you should ask, because Esme ended up coming in today, and I got her number, and I gave her an invitation to come over to my place whenever she wants. So, what do you think about that?" I crossed my arms.

Em gave me a slow clap. "Well done. See? That wasn't so hard." I'd texted her about the entire saga with Wyatt sending me the drink and the aftermath of that.

"I'm almost jealous," she said. "Esme is just so hot." She let out a dreamy sigh. "I'm so fucking single it's not even funny."

"You know we can do something about that. There're plenty of girls in this town."

Em gave me a sardonic look. "Ones that I haven't already hooked up with or dated or who aren't my type?"

I thought about that for a minute. "Okay, you may have a point."

The dating pool in town was shallow, and if you were queer, it was even more shallow. Em and I had even dated and fooled around with the same people and compared notes afterward. Awkward.

"I rest my case," Em said, leaning back in her chair. "You wanna buy me a drink and a pastry to make up for it?"

I laughed as I slid my laptop and cord into my bag. "Sure."

I STOPPED at Mom's on the way home to see how she was doing.

"You want to stay for dinner?" she asked. "I'm making fried chicken."

Who would say no to that?

"Yeah, that would be great. I can't stay too long because I have to get home to the pets." I'd been considering getting a dog for the longest time, but I'd have to hire someone to come and walk it during the day, or take it to doggie daycare, and that seemed like a huge hassle. Potato and the fish were enough for me right now.

"Sit down, sit down," she said, and I took a chair at the dining table.

I braced myself before asking, "So, how's it going?"

"Great!" she said, her voice bright. "I have *so* many people joining my team. I'm on my way to being a triple star advanced consultant." I had no idea what that meant, but I knew it was one of those bonkers ranking systems that the scam companies used to keep people sucked in. We'd done this dance before.

"Just be careful how much product you buy," I said, for the thousandth time. Could we talk about *anything* else? I was already exhausted with this.

Mom just waved me off and the conversation stalled for a little bit as she carefully dropped the chicken in the pan of oil. There was almost nothing I loved more than my mother's fried chicken. I made sure to stay out of range of the oil. I'd been burned before. Mom yammered on about local news, including a proposal for a new parking lot, one of my old teachers getting divorced, and a girl I'd gone to high school with having another baby. Mostly, I just listened and didn't have to participate too much.

Once dinner was on the table, she finally got around to asking me about my jobs, and if I was going on any dates.

"I saw Wyatt with Gretchen at the grocery store the other day. What a tramp. You should warn him about her," she said.

Was she out of her mind?

I chewed and swallowed a bite of chicken that burned my whole mouth. "I think he's well-aware by now, Mom. Besides, I'm not his keeper. He's a grown man."

"Still, he deserves better."

I put my food down. This was ridiculous. "What about me?! Don't I deserve better than him? He fucked me over, Mom. How many times do I have to tell you that?"

She set her chicken down and pursed her lips. "There's no need for language like that, Paige. I'm just saying, he was good to you while you were together. Weren't you happy? You told me you were happy."

I shouldn't have come over. Not even for the chicken. "Mom, that's not the point. In the end, he was using me and lying to me the whole time, and he dropped me like garbage. After a year. After leading me on and making me believe that I was the only one for him. He threw me away." My voice shook and I got up from the table, wiping my greasy fingers on the napkin I'd put in my lap.

"Sit down, Paige, don't go. I'm sorry, I'm sorry. Let's just have a nice dinner," she said, in her most placating tone.

I should have left. I should have made a stand. I should have not caved to pressure.

Instead, I grabbed another napkin to wipe my face and sat back down again.

"Did you hear that Haley Roberts is pregnant with twins? She's so tiny, I don't know how she's going to stay standing up," she said with a laugh, as if nothing had ever happened.

"Wow, twins," I said, and she prattled on about Haley Roberts and I finished my chicken and left the house with a box of leftovers and a pit in my stomach that had nothing to do with the food.

"I SHOULD TEXT HER," I said to Linley the next day when I stopped by the bakery. This time, she was making delicate roses to put on a birthday cake. I sat and watched as beautiful flowers bloomed while she moved the pastry bag in a circle, piping out the petals in varying shades of pink before carefully placing them on the cake with a tiny knife.

"Go ahead," she said, partially distracted by the cake.

"I don't know what to say," I said.

"Hey, you're the one who had the big plan with the cereal opening line." She turned the cake, scrutinizing it from every angle.

I looked down at my phone and chewed at my lip.

"Yeah, but that one's better delivered in person, you know? Some things don't come across as well in a text. And I need a reason to text her. The joke isn't a good enough reason. I should probably just wait."

Linley looked up and put the piping bag down. "What happened to the girl who was so confident and fired up about taking down her ex? Are you having second thoughts?"

"No. I'm not. I'm just trying to figure out the right strategy. I can't blow this." It had to be perfect, or it wasn't going to happen.

Linley's only answer was to get out a spoon, pipe some frosting onto it, and then hand me the spoon. Perfect, fluffy buttercream.

"Didn't you invite her over to your house?" she asked, as I was licking the spoon clean.

"I mean, in a general sense. I don't think she took me seriously. And she works until like 2am. I feel like we need an icebreaker first."

That was what I needed. An in.

"What was that drink she made you?" Linley asked, going back to the roses, turning the cake on its stand to make sure all the roses were evenly distributed.

"A paloma, I think." I'd made a note of it that night, and double checked.

Linley pointed the piping bag at me. "Say that you're at the store and you want to make it for yourself and ask her what's in it. Say you don't remember the name."

"Why didn't I think of that?" I asked. It was so obvious.

"Because that's what best friends are for. To see the things you can't see and point them out in loving ways." She grinned at me and went back to piping roses.

"His mom said he wanted a pink rose cake, so that's what he's getting," she muttered to herself. I got lost again in the hypnotic movement of Linley making the roses and placing them on the cake before frosting the words HAPPY BIRTHDAY SAM in beautiful cursive.

"What do you think?" she asked.

"It's beautiful. You're going to have one happy kid." Linley did a little dance and then bopped over to give me a hug.

"I'm sorry, I'm probably covered in frosting. Occupational hazard."

"No big deal," I said. "I'm used to it. In other news, tell me what's going on with Gray."

Linley smiled and let out a little giggle that I'd never heard her make.

"Well, we've been talking a lot. We're going to have an official date this weekend. We figured out a place that's almost exactly halfway between me and him and we're going to dinner and then to the movies." That sounded perfect.

"That is really cute, Lin. Like, really cute."

Her face got red and she pretended to hide behind the counter. "I knowwwwww. We're gross. But I really like him. He's so sweet and funny and I think I have a major crush. Which probably means it's too good to be true and I'm going to find out that one entire room in his house is full of ventriloquist dummies he thinks are real people, but it's so good right now."

I raised my eyebrows. "That seems like a really specific situation you're referencing, is there something you should tell me?"

She shuddered. "Not me, but a story my mom told me about a guy she met before my dad. Her cousin set her up and she was like 'never again' after that, and a week later she met my dad at the DMV, so there you go. Happy endings for everyone. I'm sure that guy is still in his home surrounded by his friends."

Picturing that was pure nightmare fuel.

"Have you asked Gray about his views on ventriloquist dummies?"

She washed her hands in the sink and then dried them. "I'm scared to."

"It's better to know sooner rather than later. That's what I didn't do with Wyatt and look at what happened to me. Learn from my mistakes."

Linley gave me a hug. "You did ignore a lot of red flags, my friend."

I sighed. "I know."

~

MY TEXT MESSAGE strategy was simple: send it while she was busy at her job so she'd be distracted and wouldn't think too much about it. Of course, that might mean I had to wait for a response, but that was fine.

I waited until dinnertime, when I figured she'd probably be well into her evening shift at the bar.

Hey, what was that drink you made me called? I want to make one.

Totally casual, totally cool. I was seriously impressed with myself.

I waited a few seconds and then decided to put my phone away so I wasn't constantly staring at it, but then she responded: **A paloma. You need lime juice, grapefruit soda, tequila, and salt. Add a dash of fresh grapefruit juice to make it really pop. If you can't find grape-fruit soda, just mix some juice with seltzer water and a little simple syrup.**

Wow, that was a lot of information. I was about to respond when she sent me a video.

My hand shook a little as I opened it.

"Hey, so here is how to make a paloma," Esme said. She was clearly in the bar, and I wondered if Batman was holding her phone as she talked through the process of making the drink, including rimming the glass with a lime wedge and then dipping it in a dish of salt to coat it. She was so fast and she did everything in a way that showed me she'd done it a hundred times before so she didn't even need to think about what she was doing. It must have been satisfying, making drinks. Knowing this alchemical process to take all these liquids and mix them in the same amounts every time to make something. My brain would not be able to remember all that.

Wow, thank you I sent after I'd watched the video five times. She didn't have to do that.

You're welcome. I figured I might as well show you, since I'm at the bar anyway.

There was a pause and then she sent another message. **If you ever need any other drink advice, let me know.**

I couldn't help but feel like she was brushing me off. Probably because she was busy.

Yeah, sure. Thanks. Have a good rest of your night.

That was probably fine for our first contact.

Doing anything fun tonight? she sent.

Oh. I guess she wasn't done with me.

Now I had to decide if I was going to tell the truth, or if I was going to try and impress her. Lying would be better, but might come back to bite me in the ass later.

Just making dinner and working.

I stared at the message and then deleted it.

Trying to decide whether I should have soup, salad, or both for dinner. Opinions?

That wasn't much more exciting, but at least it was the truth. I had a bunch of shit laid out on my counter and was desperately hoping it would make itself into something resembling food by magic instead of me having to do anything.

Both. The answer is always both.

I liked that.

Both it is.

I kept one eye on the phone and one on my fingers so I didn't chop them off as I fixed a salad of lettuce, cucumbers, tomatoes, onions, and radishes to go with some leftover turkey and rice soup I'd pulled from the freezer.

She didn't say anything while I was making the salad, which was nice because then there wasn't a ton of pressure to respond.

I washed my hands and put the soup in a pot before filling Potato's bowl.

Is work busy? I asked.

I was guessing the phone policy at the bar was pretty lax. Plus, having their bartenders post on social was a good free marketing strategy.

Always. I'm up to my eyeballs in old guys who think they have a chance. If I was from the south I'd say "bless their hearts" but I'm not, so they can just pay their tabs and leave and if they have a problem with that, they can take it up with Batman.

In addition to being a bartender, Batman also served as a bouncer when needed. The mystery of his origins and real name served to terrify even the most confident person who thought they could get away with shit because they were on vacation. Sometimes he even brought in the huge dog, and that scared people too. Interesting fellow, that Batman.

I wanted to ask her if Wyatt was there, but I didn't want to make her feel like a spy. I mean, if I really wanted to know where he was, I could check his social. I still hadn't blocked or unfollowed him anywhere for some reason.

He was probably sucking Gretchen's face off right now. Imagining it made me want to hurl.

You must get people hitting on you all the time I sent, and then wished that I hadn't. I was giving away my whole plan!

You have no idea

Fuck. I stared at my phone and then dropped it on the counter because the soup was boiling over.

Once I had dealt with that, I didn't know what else to say to her. My oh-so-brilliant line about the cereal didn't seem so brilliant anymore.

I didn't want to bug her, so I didn't say anything else while I had dinner and watched an episode of my favorite show. Potato situated himself in my lap and fell asleep.

I'd probably done enough tonight. Established the first contact and opened the line of communication. Not bad for a few text messages. I also had to leave her wanting more, and not make myself look too eager. Leave a little mystery.

∽

I WAS elbow deep in a tub of mint chip ice cream when my phone buzzed a few hours later.

You awake?

It was nearly midnight. I kept telling myself that I was staying up because there was too much to watch, but really, I'd been waiting for another text from Esme.

Yeah, but heading to bed soon.

That wasn't a lie. I did like to fall asleep before one in the morning, or else I was a mean bitch the next morning when my alarm went off.

Oh, sorry. I forget what time it is for normal people. I keep vampire hours.

She would make such a sexy vampire I thought, but didn't send that to her.

It's okay. I don't mind. What's up? I asked.

She typed something and then deleted it, then spent a long time typing something else. I had to stop staring at those little dots moving while she figured out what to send. Maybe she just got distracted by something else. It was hard to tell.

I wish you were here so I could make you a paloma instead of my millionth Jager bomb she finally sent.

Oh.

I wish I was there too. Except that would mean I'd have to put pants back on.

Shit, that was probably too much. I couldn't seem to help myself from blurting out whatever I thought, even in texts.

Hey, you haven't seen some of the people in here. Pants are nice, but definitely not a requirement. She sent that with a little winking emoji. I shuddered, thinking about what she must have seen before.

Should I even ask? I sent.

Her next message was a voice memo. "Probably not. I've seen enough butts to last a lifetime. What is it about some people deciding to take their clothes off when they get drunk? And don't get me started on how many times people thought this was the Coyote Ugly bar and they could dance on top of it. Let's just say I've had to call for an ambulance more than once." She had to speak loudly over the noise of the bar, but it was still nice to hear her voice.

She sent a second message. "I just want to go home and not talk to anyone else for like a week, and not smile. My face gets tired of smiling." She sighed.

You should go on a stoic vacation. Give your face and voice a week off. Run off and rent a cabin in the middle of the woods.

Honestly, that sounded amazing. If I didn't always bring my work with me, I would have done the same thing.

"That sounds like heaven, honestly," she said.

I closed my eyes for a minute and imagined what it would be like. I could just read and sit still and not answer emails or texts or phone calls. No meetings. No deadlines. Maybe I'd finally teach myself how to knit. Obviously, I'd bring several puzzles. I had a new one coming in a few days. The puzzle table in the corner of my living room was clear and ready to go.

"Shit, one of my regulars is talking about his ex-wife. That's only going to lead to a lot of crying, so I need to cut him off and get him home. Have a good night, Paige."

She should have been a therapist. I bet she would have made more money. Less debt as a bartender, though.

Oh no, that sounds like a lot. Have a good rest of your night, Esme.

And that was that. Hopefully she'd still want to talk to me tomorrow.

Chapter Five

THE NEXT DAY, I stopped at the grocery store to grab a few things, and I found myself drifting toward the alcohol aisle. I didn't drink much, just socially, but I couldn't get the memory of the drink Esme had made for me out of my head. I put a random bottle of tequila in my cart and then went in search of the other ingredients.

On my way, I bumped into my third-grade teacher, the nurse at my doctor's office, my mom's lawyer, and I ended up having to hide from Wyatt and Emerald's mom.

She and I had gotten pretty close when he and I had dated, and I missed her, but I couldn't see her without wanting to tell her how much of a fucking fuck her son was. Like, it wasn't her fault that he was the way he was, but I wondered if she ever talked to him about his behavior, or if she just let it go. Wyatt walked around with the kind of energy that everyone he'd ever encountered had let him get away with shit and he'd never been told no. Weird, because Em wasn't like that at all. I guess I didn't understand those kinds of sibling dynamics. I was an only child.

I thought I was safe, but then I got in line to check out and was putting my items on the conveyor belt and heard my name. Foolishly, I turned to find Katherine Witmer giving me a big smile that reminded me so much of Wyatt, it was like a punch in the chest.

"Hey," I said. "Um, hi." I forced my hands to keep putting things from my cart on the belt.

"How are you doing?" She seemed completely fine, which made me feel even more weird. I kept dropping things and I was so flustered that I was sure everyone could tell.

I wanted a hole to open up in the floor and suck me in. Why was this happening?

"I'm fine," I said, because what else was I going to say?

"Good, good," she said, and I noticed just a little bit of tightness around her eyes as she smiled at me again. "It's nice to see you. Say hello to your mother for me."

She'd been waiting behind me, but she got out of line to go to another register, which made me think she wasn't as composed as I'd originally thought. Maybe she did know what her son was like?

Somehow, I got through the rest of the process without any further embarrassment, but it was a close thing. I really needed a vacation from my life.

"SAW YOUR MOM TODAY," I said later, when I was hanging out with Em. She also had the misfortune of still living with her parents (albeit in an apartment above the garage, but still), so she escaped to my house when she could.

"Yeah? Did she say anything?"

I set down the knife I'd been using to cut lime wedges for our drinks. I'd texted her earlier about making the drinks and she'd been game.

"I mean, not really. Then she kind of ran away, so it was weird for everyone involved." I cringed.

"Ugh, I'm sorry. My brother sucks."

I sighed. "Yeah, he does. I wish I would have seen it sooner."

"Do you want me to give you an update on him?" She asked, leaning on the counter.

I had to think about that. "No. I don't want to know." I went back to cutting the limes.

"Okay, so we need to rim the glass, and then pour it in the right order," I said. I had my phone propped up on the tequila bottle and Esme's video playing on a loop.

"Can I do the salt part?" Em asked. "I don't know why, but that seems like the most fun part."

"Sure." I let her add salt to the glasses and then poured everything in, mixed it, and added ice.

"I don't have a shaker, so whatever," I said. "I couldn't find one in the store and there wasn't time to order one."

Em picked up her glass and I grabbed mine.

"Cheers," I said. We both drank and it wasn't the same as the one Esme had made me, but it was still good.

"Not bad," I said. "If I'm not careful, I'll drink this too fast."

"Same. I have to drive home, so I should take it slow."

We parked ourselves on my couch and Potato betrayed me to sit with Em and get ear rubs. I'd also brought over a tray of snacks for us to amuse ourselves with post-dinner.

"Why is it only Thursday? This is bullshit," she said.

"Oh, it's Thursday?" I very often forgot what day of the week it was. Since I worked all the time, I forgot that regular people worked Monday through Friday.

"Yes, and I wish it was Friday so I didn't have to go in tomorrow. It's Casual Friday and we have a team-building meeting." She gave me a fake smile.

"I have never been to one of those, but they sound like nightmares," I said.

"They are all of that and more. Remind me to tell you about the time when we had to take a personality test based on which animal we were, and then try and socialize wearing animal masks. I escaped to the bathroom and pretended I had food poisoning from Patricia's macaroni casserole."

I shoved a handful of popcorn in my mouth and almost choked. "From what I've heard about Patricia's casserole, that wouldn't have been far from the truth."

Em tilted her drink in my direction. "You're right there."

"Sometimes I do wish I could have office small talk. That seems fun. A group chat isn't the same thing."

Em groaned. "It's not. Believe me. It's awful. I would love to never do it again."

I let her bitch about how much she hated her job because she didn't really have a whole lot of friends around here. She'd had a hard time differentiating herself from her brother, and she didn't want to hang out with the same people. Unfortunately, that meant that she didn't want to hang out with the majority of the twenty-somethings in Castleton. There was a whole big group of townies that got together for bonfires and garage parties and any other excuse to sit around and talk about other times they got drunk while they got drunk again.

Sure, I'd gone a few times, but once you've heard one story, you've heard them all. Just not my kind of people. Plus, Wyatt was basically their king, and now that we weren't together, I didn't want to be anywhere he was if I could help it.

Em got a text from her dad to head home because he didn't want her to be tired for work, so she rolled her eyes and got up.

"I swear, they are never going to treat me like I'm grown. My brother was allowed to go on a plane by himself when he was twelve, but if I'm home a few minutes later than I said I was going to be, they lose their minds and think I'm dead." I gave her a hug and let her know that she could crash at my place on the couch anytime she wanted to get away, and I'd see her on Saturday to collect shells.

"One more day," she said with a sigh. "One more day."

I started humming the tune "One Day More" from Les Mis and she slammed her hands over her ears.

"Don't, now I'll have that stuck in my head, lalalala," she said in a loud voice, and started running for the door as I increased my singing in volume and intensity.

By the time she was in her car, I was standing in the doorway with my arm raised, belting it at full volume as Em shook her head and backed out of the driveway.

AFTER SHE LEFT, I made myself another paloma and then spent like a half an hour trying to take a decent picture of it and failing a bunch.

My best attempt I sent to Esme.

Looks great! Make me one?

She probably got so tired of making drinks for people. Anything got tedious if you did it for enough times as a job. I wanted to tell her to come get one when she was off work, but she would probably think I was only joking. And I didn't know if I was ready for her to see my house yet. We needed to meet on neutral ground first.

You got it I said.

A few minutes later I got another voice memo: "I'm hiding in the employee bathroom right now because I don't want to talk to another person. I mean, I'm talking to you right now but that's different. You're not customer and I'm not forced by capitalism to serve you with a smile on my face."

THE WORST I sent back. I preferred texting because recording my voice felt too intimate.

She sent back: "Sorry, I'm grouchy. I feel like I'm always complaining to you. Are you doing anything fun this weekend?"

Trying to force myself to not work, and I'm going to the beach with Emerald to find shells. She makes all kinds of cool things out of them. Definitely reading. You? I didn't add that I would also definitely be putting in some quality puzzle time. It was just too silly a hobby to share with her just yet. I wanted her to think of me as sexy, not as a person who did puzzles while watching *Murder, She Wrote*.

She replied: "Mostly working, but Dad is pestering me to go out and have some fun, so who knows. My idea of fun and other people's idea of fun are two different things."

What is fun for you? I really wanted to know. She probably had all kinds of interesting hobbies like taxidermy or necromancy.

She said: "You're going to think I'm a total dork, but whatever. I'm over apologizing for the shit that I like. I have a website where I do book recommendations, and I also love to collect rare books. I don't have any particular interest there, but I have a ton of weird things that no one else wanted." She laughed. "If it's a little twisted or dark or offbeat, I'll probably love it."

Oh. I didn't know that.

I sent her back the title of the last book I'd read, a historical romance that was in a series about rakes who ran an underground gaming club. My reading tastes were all over the place. The book I'd finished before that was a non-fiction book about Chernobyl.

"Maybe I'll have to give it a try," she sent.

Yeah, let me know what you think.

"I should probably get back to the bar or Batman is going to get in over his head. I love him, but he can't handle a rush on his own. It was really nice talking to you, Paige."

It was nice talking to you. Have a good rest of your night.

"Have a good rest of your week."

I slumped back on the couch and realized I'd been sweating the whole time and now I was totally overhead. I went to open the window and turn on a fan to get some air circulating in the cottage.

I'd done it. I'd had a full conversation with her. I made myself another paloma to celebrate.

Chapter Six

"So, what's the next part of your plan?" Em asked, as we picked our way over wet rocks strewn with seaweed, hoping to find empty mussel shells for her to use in her crafts. During the summer, there were a hell of a lot more people looking for shell souvenirs, so it was a lot harder to get a good haul. So far, we only had a handful in her mesh bag.

I stood up and stretched my back. "I'm doing more of a slow seduction. A slowduction. I feel like jumping her would backfire. Plus, flirting with her in public where Wyatt might see is going to do way more damage than hooking up with her behind closed doors."

Em nodded and threw a shell in the bag slung around her shoulder. "That makes sense. Giving Wyatt the mass amount of suffering is really paramount. Speaking of that, I've been pushing his buttons for you."

I pushed some seaweed aside that hung in front of a rock and met the beady eyes of a grumpy crab. I covered them back up and moved on.

"What do you mean?" I asked.

"Oh, I've been subtly talking about Esme and trying to get

him to talk about her. He's not the brightest, so I don't think he has any idea what I'm doing. So like, I'll pretend I just happened to see her post on social and be like 'remember when you tried to ask her out?' He got pissed and ran to Gretchen's."

She grinned and I felt an answering smile on my face.

"Nice." Wyatt had not failed with Esme just once. Oh no. He had failed many, many times over the years, starting when he was a young teenager. He didn't know that I knew about all his failures, because his sister had told me. My favorite was when he made an elaborate set-up to ask her to prom and she just rejected him in front of the entire school. It was a wonder he didn't hate her for it. Nope, it only made him want her more.

"How are he and Gretchen?" It physically hurt me to say her name.

Em and I moved to a new section of rocks, and I got completely lost staring into a tidepool as seagulls wheeled overhead and called to each other.

"Ugh, disgusting. He brought her over for dinner and I had to smile and be nice and try not to stab her with a fork when she tried to kiss my mom's ass. Fortunately, Mom saw right through her bullshit. I have no idea why she can't see through her son's, but whatever. She told me afterward that she thinks Gretchen is 'a nice girl, but definitely a gold digger.'"

I thought about that for a second. "Yeah, from what I know about her character, it wouldn't surprise me." Em's mom had her own accounting firm, and her dad was a VP at his brother's insurance company. They had an in-ground pool and hot tub, in Maine, which, in our small town, meant you had to be loaded.

Wyatt pretended he had a job when it suited him, but he played a lot of golf and went to a lot of "business lunches" and was always coming up with some new business idea every six months. His parents would give him the cash, he'd crash and burn, and then lather, rinse, repeat. Blah, blah, blah. He was the definition of "failing upwards."

Whenever I questioned why the hell I had fallen in love with him, I had to remind myself that sometimes I made bad decisions and that didn't mean I was a bad person. Plus, you know, the sex.

I really needed to stop thinking about fucking Wyatt or else I was going to text him and tell him to come over for a little throwback Thursday.

"Paige?" Em waved her hand in front of my face. "Where did you go?"

"I was remembering fucking your brother," I said, and she made gagging noises.

"Don't ever say anything like that to me again or I'm tossing you in the ocean."

I shrugged. "You forget I swim in the ocean all the time. It's actually warm right now." There were only a handful of humans swimming in the water, and a whole lot who dipped their toes in, screamed at the temperature, and then decided to go sit on their towels in the sun instead. I'd worn my suit under my shorts and tank, so I was going to take a dip before I left.

"Fine, but don't talk about my brother's sex life ever again. There is not enough brain bleach in the entire world." She shuddered.

"Anything else about Gretchen? Is he really into her, or is she one of the only girls he hasn't destroyed yet?" Honestly, I really should befriend Wyatt's other exes. I used to see them as potential enemies when I'd dated him. A few had even tried to warn me about him, but he did that thing where he said they were just "crazy bitches" and I let him gaslight me. I wanted to reach into the past and slap some sense into myself.

"Too soon to tell," Em said, carefully climbing over a rock

to make sure she didn't slip. "She doesn't seem like the sharpest cookie in the drawer."

I stared at her for a second. "I don't think that's the expression."

"Well, it's my expression."

I snorted and sat down on a rock and tilted my face toward the sun. I probably should have worn a hat, but at least I'd remembered sunblock. In my teen years I'd been all about getting a tan as quickly as possible in the summer, but now I knew better.

"She keeps trying to butter up my mom, but I keep reminding her that Gretchen used to cyberbully me online."

"Wait, you too?" I thought I'd been one of the only ones.

"I think that's what she did instead of homework."

The water in the little tidepool next to me sparkled and distracted me. Such a beautiful little ecosystem. Hermit crabs, tiny shrimp, snails, and even a few small fish all hung out together in harmony. A movement caught my eye and a baby lobster peeked out from behind some seaweed.

"Hey, baby lobster," I said, and Em came over to take a look. Seeing one this small close to shore was rare.

"Someday I may eat you with butter," Em said in a baby voice.

"Don't listen to her," I called to the lobster.

The lobster ignored both of us.

The two of us meandered to the sandy part of the beach in search of more shells. The tide was starting to come back in, so we had limited time to search for treasures.

"Wow," Em said, and I looked up.

"What?"

"Her," she said, jerking her chin at a woman walking toward the ocean ahead of us. "Hot."

"Not my type, but I can see it." The woman had a teeny tiny bikini on, and it was clear she spent some time and effort to look the way she did. Like, congratulations to you, but I'd feel like a gross blob in comparison. She looked like she stepped out of a social media campaign for sunglasses or abs or something.

"I would top her so hard," Em said in a wistful voice.

"Been a while?" I asked, and she grimaced.

"You have no idea. I can't even remember what I'm supposed to do. I swear, I'm going to eventually get with someone and be like 'how do you sex?'"

We both laughed. "You'll figure it out, I promise."

"Maybe I won't. Maybe I'll never have sex with another person again." She said that in a louder voice than she probably intended, and we got angry glares from a mom who was making a sandcastle with her toddler.

"Don't talk about sex that loudly in public, Em," I said, and she rolled her eyes.

"See? I can't even talk about it like a normal person."

AFTER EM LEFT, I found three pieces of beach glass, which was rare. I shoved the little bits in my shorts pocket before stripping down to my suit and walking toward the ocean. There were two ways to get in the water: Either go in a little at a time, letting your body adjust, or diving in and shocking yourself completely.

I was a fan of the second method.

The bone-chilling water closed over my head and my body had a moment of panic, but I resurfaced and tried to remind my lungs how to work. After a few moments, I could breathe again and get my arms to work. I started doing my laps from one end of the beach to the other. My lungs and heart and legs and arms were all moving and it was such a relief to not think about anything but the exercise. I swam until the shivers in my body took over and I knew I needed a hot shower to get back to normal.

Before I left, I took a picture of the beach and posted it on my social media with a silly caption.

Three minutes later, Esme liked it.

LINLEY TEXTED me after I got home that she was just leaving to go on her date with Gray. She gave me the location, and the go ahead that if I didn't hear from her in a few hours, to call the cops because she might have been murdered.

FUNNY. But seriously, be safe. I sent.

She said she would, and she also relayed that her mom had asked if she could video her entire date so she could "meet" Gray.

I need to ease him in. She's basically already decided we're getting married. I swear I caught her looking for cake toppers the other day.

I felt bad for Linley, but I also was grateful my own mother didn't pull shenanigans like that. No, mine just joined pyramid schemes and begged me to win back my ex-boyfriend. I couldn't decide which was worse.

Bored in the house, I decided that I didn't feel like cooking, so I finger-combed my damp hair, put on a tank and a comfy jumpsuit, and headed over to the Pine State Bar and Grill.

Dawn seated me on the opposite side of the restaurant from the bar, so I couldn't see Esme at all. My plan was to eat dinner and go for a drink later and do some serious flirting.

Craving seafood after the day at the beach, I ordered the shrimp and haddock basket with fries so hot and fresh they burned my fingers when I tried to eat them.

I sucked down a half-lemonade, half-iced tea and hurried through the rest of my food. I paid my tab and made my way to the bar. Esme had dark purple lipstick on tonight, leather shorts, and a faded and ripped black t-shirt. She looked like she'd come from a rock concert, and I looked down at my own outfit.

I looked like a toddler who'd escaped from daycare. What the hell was I thinking? Blushing, I started to back away and leave before she could see me, but it didn't work.

"Paige! You here for a drink?" Esme beamed at me as she wiped out a glass.

"Uh, sure?" I said, as if I wasn't sure. There was an empty barstool in front of me, and I let myself fall onto it.

Esme leaned over on the bar, her eyes sparkling in the light of several neon beer signs. I swear, I didn't even need a drink to feel intoxicated around her.

"Would you like a paloma, or something else? Maybe a mocktail? I make amazing mocktails."

"Sure, I'd love one."

Esme winked at me and I almost fell to the floor. "You got it."

She moved so fast that I couldn't even track what she was doing. Esme added ice to a glass, poured some liquid from a jar that she strained beforehand, topped it with something, and put a lime wedge on the side. The whole thing was a beautiful dance, done by someone who'd honed her skills.

She slid the glass in front of me. "Let me know what you think. This is fun, getting to try drinks on someone."

The drink smelled like pineapple, but it also smelled spicy, so I had no idea, but I was up for trying it.

I took one sip as Esme hovered, waiting for my verdict. Initially, the drink was sweet, and definitely flavored with pineapple. Then I swallowed and was hit with a kick of heat.

"Holy shit," I said, coughing a little.

She leaned even further forward. "Sorry, is a little strong?"

I shook my head, trying to get my breath back. "No, it's

just that I wasn't expecting it." The spiciness sat on my tongue and dulled as I waited. Wow. I took another sip and this time I was prepared and didn't choke.

"Holy shit, that is good." My tongue burned, but I wasn't going to stop drinking it.

"Good. It's got peppercorns and chiles in it. As well as pineapple and lime." She was really hitting me hard with the incredible drinks lately.

"No, it's so good." Since there was no booze in it, I could suck this one down and just ask her for another when I wanted it.

Other customers snagged her attention and she had to leave me and go tend to them, so I sat and sipped my drink and watched her work while also pretending to be watching whatever the hell was happening on the TVs mounted on the wall if she ever looked in my direction. Not an easy feat.

The bar filled up and I was squished between a few people who didn't understand personal space. If I wasn't here for Esme, I wasn't sure I would voluntarily come here as an alternative to being at home on my couch where I didn't have to smell someone else's perfume or cologne. Plus, my cat was there.

"What are you smiling about?" Esme said, diving out of Batman's way as he dumped a massive bucket of ice into a cooler.

"Oh, nothing."

"No, tell me." I would have told her anything if she asked me when she looked at me like that. Like she was interested in what I had to say.

"I was thinking about what my cat would do if he was here. Probably walk along the bar and knock all the drinks off. Or bite a bunch of people for not giving him treats." Potato loved me, but he was a prickly fellow and didn't trust other people.

Esme chuckled. "That sounds cute. His name is Potato, right?"

For the second time, I almost fell off my stool. How did she know my cat's name?

"Yeah, it is."

She must have seen the look on my face because she said, "I've seen you post about him on your social."

Oh, right. We followed each other. She'd probably been looking at my posts. Obviously. *Get a grip, Paige.*

"He's so cute. I'd love to get a cat, but I don't think Stormy would like it. She's too much of a drama queen. Maybe I could come visit your cat." This was the second time she'd talked about coming over, and I didn't think it was reading too much into things to make the leap that she actually did want to come over to my house.

"When's your next day off?" I asked, after I finished my drink.

"Uhhhh, what is today?" she asked. I told her was Saturday. "Tuesday."

I had a huge deadline for an annoying project on Wednesday that I had already blocked out most of the day to tackle. But, if I busted my butt a little bit tomorrow, and on Monday, I could squeeze in some free hours in the middle of the day.

"I have to work, but I can make some time in the afternoon," I said, and she took my glass and made me another drink without even asking if I wanted one. I did.

"You don't have to skip work for me," she said, setting it down in front of me. I picked up the slippery glass and took another sip. So damn good.

"No, it's cool, I always take a break in the early afternoon. Just come over whenever." That sounded cool and casual, even though both my legs were trembling under the cover of the bar.

"You sure?" she asked as she wiped the bar in front of me with a warm rag that smelled faintly of bleach.

"Yeah, of course. Come on over. I'll try and make sure Potato doesn't bite you." He'd better be nice to her, or I was going to be cross with him.

"Will he like me if I bring him treats?"

"He is the pickiest cat I've ever met, so let me just send you the exact kind. I get them at your dad's store, actually." I found the link and sent it to her.

"He's not picky, he just knows what he wants," she said, looking into my eyes. It was suddenly hard to swallow.

"Yeah," I said, but I didn't know what I was responding to. I'd completely forgotten what we'd been talking about.

She had to leave me again and go help Batman, so I sat and sipped my second drink. I couldn't linger too long here. Mystery. Always leave with an air of mystery. Too bad I didn't have a cape that I could swirl dramatically on my exit.

Batman shuffled over and gave me a smile and I told him I wanted to close out my tab. He ran my card as Esme dealt with a group down the end of the bar who was having a *very* good time, if I could judge by the volume of their laughter. She laughed along with them as she poured another round of shots. I gave her one last glance before I stood up and headed out to my car.

~

WHERE DID YOU GO? **I turned around and you weren't there anymore.**

I got the text just as I was walking into the house and saying hello to Potato.

Sorry! You seemed busy and I had to come feed this monster. I took a picture of Potato screaming at me and sent it to her.

Well we can't have a starving kitty! It was good to see you tonight, Paige.

Heat rushed to my face. I sat down and wondered what to say to that. Giving up on being creative, I went with simple.

It was good to see you too. I hope you get lots of tips tonight.

She sent a laughing emoji. **Not likely, but thanks for the good vibes anyway.**

Potato rolled onto his back and showed me his belly floof, begging for pets. I took a quick video of him while I gave him what he wanted and then sent it to Esme.

He doesn't look like he'd bite anyone she sent back. As I was reading the text, Potato gently nipped at my hand to let me know I wasn't petting him correctly.

I didn't want to throw him under the bus, or make her scared of him, so I didn't.

Goodnight, Paige.

'Night, Esme.

Chapter Seven

"TELL ME LITERALLY EVERYTHING," I said to Linley the next day when I went over to her place. Clearly the date had gone well, because she had slept in and was still yawning and disheveled when I knocked on her door after she'd buzzed me up.

Linley smiled and then tried to hide it as she set a cup of coffee in front of me and shoved a plate with a piece of heirloom tomato quiche on it toward me.

"I can't tell you *everything*," she said, pulling her legs up onto her chair and setting her cup of coffee on her knees. "But it was good. It was *really* good." She couldn't stop smiling.

"You totally got laid. I'm so jealous." I hadn't had sex since Wyatt, and even though it wasn't that long, it felt like much longer. It wasn't just the sex part that I missed. It was the stuff that accompanied sex. Cuddling naked with another body, having deep conversations that you might not have in normal circumstances, a post-coital shower. The intimacy. My skin craved to be touched.

"I mean, we didn't have sex in his car, but we did do some things." Her face got red.

"Was it good?"

She bit her bottom lip and her cheeks got redder. "Oh yeah. He has very talented hands. He has a hobby carving miniature wooden animals." That was absolutely adorable.

"Can I see?" I asked.

She gave me a weird look.

I clarified. "*The stuff he carves.* I don't need to see his hands." Although, I did like a nice set of hands. Forearms too. Mmmmm.

While I finished my coffee and quiche, Linley showed me Gray's social media page and his online shop. His work was absolutely incredible.

"Wow, this is so impressive," I said, scrolling through page after page of lifelike animals that he posed outside on a stump with acorns for scale.

"Yeah, he's been doing it since he was in college. His grandfather taught him to carve and he's been doing these guys. He'll do a drop of a limited edition one and they sell out in like a few hours."

"Very cool. Now tell me about the sex."

Linley groaned, but gave me the dirty details.

"So, when are you going to see him again?" I asked.

"Well, we've been texting and we have a video chat for tonight." She could not stop smiling, and it was so great to see.

"Have you told your mom yet?"

Linley snorted into her coffee. "I didn't tell her about the sexy stuff, but she knows that the date was great and I really like him. It's still early, I know, but it feels good."

She was glowing, and it wasn't because a cute boy had touched her boobs in the backseat of his car.

"I bet he's carving you a little animal right now," I said. "If he doesn't, you should ask him to. Request something weird like a wombat or a pangolin."

"A pangolin?"

"Yeah, you know what a pangolin is."

She shook her head.

"Oh my god, okay." I pulled up pictures of pangolins and showed them to her.

"Aw, they look so nervous. I love it," she said. "I'm totally sending one to Gray."

"I'm telling you. He's going to show up at your next date with a carved pangolin. I would put money on it."

I was completely and totally happy for my friend. But that little tiny whisper of jealousy wouldn't go away. I missed feeling the way she felt. The energy and fizzy happiness of a new relationship. Where every single message or call made you giddy.

"You want to take a walk?" I asked. There was a sweet ocean breeze that swept away the heat from the pavement outside.

"Yeah, sure." I helped her clean the dishes before we headed out to my car to drive the short distance to the nature preserve with a trail running through it that would offer some shade from the sun, and a little bit of distance from the many tourists clogging the streets in town.

"It's times like these when I wish I had a dog. They should have a service where you can rent someone else's dog and take it out for a few hours and then give it back," Linley said, as we parked in the little lot at the head of the trail. I threw my water bottle in my bag and put it on.

"I mean, I think that's just like, being a dog walker. You could do that."

"If I wasn't so damn exhausted from working full-time, I would."

"You really do need to cut your hours back. Maybe now that you're seeing Gray, you could pitch that you need more time for dating so you can convince him to be your husband." I wiggled my eyebrows suggestively.

"You know what? That is not a bad idea."

I thought it was pretty good. She needed to talk to her parents, but I got how hard it was. She wanted to support them, and they relied on her, but she needed to set some better boundaries. To be honest, I thought it wasn't as big a deal as she was making it. Her parents were good people. They didn't want her to be unhappy or overworked.

"I don't know if he's going to be my husband, but I'm not thinking that far ahead. I can't put that much pressure on something so new. Like, I could find out he's a shitty person, or that he doesn't want kids, or anything else. It might not work out, so I'm not putting all my eggs in the Gray basket."

"Even if the basket is really hot," I added, and she laughed.

"He *is* really hot, isn't he?"

"Totally. Good-looking and interesting? Sexy combination."

Linley made a whining noise. "He's just so smart and so hot and I'm trying to keep myself from liking him too much too fast, help."

We kept walking and I told her that she couldn't really stop her feelings from existing, but that she should definitely learn from my many dating mistakes. I had made so many of them in such a short amount of time. I hadn't dated much in high school. It seemed like a lot of work, and I was dealing with a lot of messy feelings at the time. Hooking up and keeping things casual was much easier. Didn't stop me from falling in love every other week and getting my heart broken a bunch of times, though, so I guess it wasn't that good of a plan.

"But enough about me, how goes the progress with Esme?" Linley said.

"Slower than I'd like, but it's going. I'm seeing her on Tuesday. She's coming over to hang out with Potato." It sounded ridiculous when I said it out loud, but it didn't seem like a bad start.

"You're using your grumpy cat to seduce her? I mean, at least it's creative. Better than the cereal thing."

We reached the end of the trail, which was just before a small and rocky beach. You couldn't really go swimming or anything like that, but it was still nice to be by the water. The two of us trudged on the rocks along with lots of other people, including several families with kids that kept trying to sneak away and get in the water. I didn't blame them. I was wishing I'd worn a suit under my hiking clothes and brought a towel.

"Want to sit?" I asked, and we parked ourselves on one side of the beach and lay down in the sun.

"So, what are your big plans when Esme comes over? You going to just whip a boob out?"

I opened my eyes and looked over at her. "Is that what you did with Gray? No wonder he wants to keep seeing you."

She smacked me in the shoulder. "No, but what's the strategy?"

"I'm just going to play it by ear. I'll get nervous if I think about it too much. This is more like laying groundwork than anything. I'm not like Wyatt, trying to get into her pants immediately. I'm all about the slow seduction."

"Okay, so take out a boob slowly."

"Linley!" I said. "There are children around."

"Children know about boobs."

I laughed and lay back on the sun-warmed rock.

"I still think my boob idea is good," Linley grumbled.

I WAS EXHAUSTED from my hike, but I needed to get ahead on work, and I needed to check on my mom. After I dropped Linley off, I went home to shower and then see Mom.

"Hey, what are you doing here?" she asked when I walked into the living room and found her on her laptop.

"Just came over to see you," I said, leaning down and giving her a hug. "What's going on?"

"I'm working on my social media," she said with a smile. "Take a look!"

I'd been down this road before with her. She would get all pumped up and sometimes sink money into marketing schemes and then lose momentum and get distracted a month later. In the beginning I'd tried to help her, but she didn't want my help anymore, so the only thing I could do was hope she came to her senses before she lost too much money. I just wish she could find something to do with her time that wasn't a terrible waste.

"Looks great, Mom," I said, my eyes aching after looking at the terrible stock images run through a disgusting filter that littered her page, along with inspirational quotes.

"Hey, I saw there was a flyer for a new mystery book club at the library. You love true crime. You should join it." There was one thing my mom loved as much as joining one network marketing company after another, and that was true crime. I'd grown up with her watching movies with me that I was probably much too young to see and giving me nightmares about scary dudes coming in my window to snatch me away for nefarious purposes.

"Maybe," she said in a disinterested tone. Hey, at least I tried.

"Linley is seeing someone new." That got her attention.

"Tell me everything," she said.

I told her the details of the date, omitting the sexier stuff, of course. There were just some lines I didn't want to cross with my mom, thank you.

"He doesn't have any friends or brothers?" she asked when I was done. Of course.

"I don't know, I'll find out," I said, in a deadpan voice.

"Just think how perfect it would be," she said, grabbing my hands. "You could have a double wedding."

Wow. My mom was just as bad as Linley's. It was weird they weren't better friends, but they stayed mostly cordial with each other and always had been. My mom burned so many friendship bridges, and to be honest, she was a lot.

"I think that's a little premature, but I'll see how Linley feels about it," I said, but I wasn't serious.

Mom made me some tea and nagged me some more and by the time I got home I was drained, but then I had a cup of coffee and revived myself with a quick chicken Caesar salad and a fresh mango I ate over the sink.

I hated working Sundays, but it was a sacrifice for a good cause. I also needed to remember to clean my house. Yes, my house was cleanish now, but it wasn't company clean.

I also needed to plan an outfit and have snacks on hand. This seduction business was a lot of work. I was already tired. Dating hadn't been this much work, or at least not the way I'd been doing it. Wyatt hadn't expected charcuterie and sparkling conversation. He usually just wanted to eat pizza off my tits after we fucked or something. He also hadn't really noticed when I'd gotten spruced up for him, so I'd stopped trying. For someone who was so conscious about image, he hadn't seemed worried about mine, which was confusing.

I had to impress Esme. I had to get her to like me. To want to keep spending time with me. And I didn't think she was going to be so easily swayed by nudity. I guess I'd figure that out on Tuesday.

Potato jumped on my lap and tried to push the laptop onto the floor, but I moved it out of the way so he didn't wreak havoc on my work.

"Do you need attention?" I asked him, and he started kneading the blanket that I placed between myself and my laptop so my body didn't overheat.

"Okay then." I put my laptop on the coffee table and gave him snuggles for a while.

"Are you going to be mean to Esme? You'd better not bite her," I said to him.

He just blinked at me, stretched his front paws out, and fell asleep.

～

MONDAY WAS a whirlwind of emails back and forth and back and forth and trying to get myself caught up. I powered through and worked past my normal time so that I had breathing room for my afternoon with Esme. When I finally closed my laptop for the day, I ran around shoving things in cabinets and wiping down my counters and dusting my knick-knacks. The house wasn't that bad in the first place, but I wanted it to look good. I wanted her to like it. This was the first place I'd really gotten to make my own and I'd splattered my personality in every nook and cranny.

After a quick shower, I fell into bed and was already dreading my alarm, but I was ready. I'd even given Potato an extra-long brushing session so his coat was looking fluffy and fabulous.

～

TUESDAY I WOKE up to my alarm with a start, as if I'd forgotten something. When my brain finally cleared, I realized that today was my afternoon with Esme. Shit. I got up and made myself breakfast and wiped down the kitchen again before starting work. It seemed like a waste of time to go to the café just for a short time, so I set myself up on the couch with my headphones.

Between the distractions of being in my home, and worrying about Esme coming over, I got just about nothing done. I couldn't stop checking the time on my phone.

You still cool to hang out? I sent while I ate leftover salad in the kitchen. I hadn't heard from Esme to confirm a time yet, and I didn't want to be weirdo, but I also needed to mentally prepare myself.

Both Linley and Em would probably tell me I was worrying about nothing, but Esme was still so hard to read. I couldn't make sense of her. I couldn't tell if she was just being nice, or if she was really into me. I needed more signals! Things had been so easy with Wyatt, and most of the other people I'd dated. They'd taken the lead because I guess I was kind of oblivious. Me being the pursuer was something new and I basically didn't know what I was doing.

Get it together, Paige.

Yeah, I'll be there around 1:15, is that good?

That gave me a half hour to do another sweep of the house, put on my outfit, and make sure I looked good. I actually put on foundation and filled in my brows and clipped part of my hair back. I had to admit, I looked cute as hell. I just hoped that Esme liked cute.

I fiddled with my t-shirt for at least ten minutes before there was a knock at the door.

Potato ran into the bedroom to look at me and then back out to the living room to see what was going on.

"We've got a visitor. She's here to see you just as much as she's here to see me."

I opened the door and forgot how to speak.

"Hey," she said, standing there wearing a pair of black jeans that were ripped to hell and a purple crop top. Her hair was down, as usual, and it glowed in the sunshine, showing the subtle dark red highlights. She held out a bouquet of flowers to me.

She looked fucking incredible and I wanted to crawl under the couch.

"Wow," I said, before I could stop myself. "Sorry, hi." All

of the blood in my body rushed immediately to my face. I was doing great so far.

"Dad lets Dora Mimms set up her flower cart in the parking lot every week, so I grabbed these for you."

I somehow made my arms move and take the bouquet of delicate baby pink roses from her.

It took me another two seconds at least to realize that I had to move aside to let her in. I was still dying a little when Potato ran over to see what the ruckus was about.

"Oh, hello pretty boy." Esme leaned down and held out her hand to him. He ran right up to her, gave her hand a few sniffs and then bonked it with his head.

"Yes, you're a sweetheart. You would never bite anyone," she crooned at him as he purred so loudly I bet the neighbors could hear. Esme found the special spot under his chin that he really loved and then he was rolling on the ground and begging for belly rubs.

"I think I've been replaced," I said, and sneakily tried to sniff the flowers, even though I knew they probably didn't smell like anything. "I should get these in some water. Come on in."

Esme followed me into the kitchen where I found one of my cut glass vases that I'd gotten at an estate sale ages ago. I almost forgot to trim the stems before adding them to the water.

"They're beautiful, thank you so much," I said.

"You're welcome."

No romantic partner had ever gotten me flowers before. Not even Wyatt on Valentine's Day. He'd claimed that big displays like flowers and candy was for losers, and instead gave me mind-blowing sex. Sure, the sex was great, but I also would have liked some flowers and a heart-shaped box of chocolates.

"Can I get you anything? I have snacks and stuff." That was putting it mildly. I had a whole ass charcuterie plate wrapped up in the fridge that I'd painstakingly arranged. I'd thought about buying one but decided to give it a try myself and I'd had a little too much fun making it.

"Yeah, sure, whatever you have. I don't want to impose."

"You're not imposing, I invited you over." I went to the fridge and pulled out a few different drink options, including beer. She took a can of seltzer water and I copied her.

"Thanks."

Potato meowed and wound himself around her legs, begging for treats.

"Don't worry, I brought something for you," Esme said, pulling a bag of his favorite treats from her back pocket. Potato was instantly on the alert at the telltale crinkle of the bag and put his paws on Esme's legs to try and reach to bat the bag out of her hand.

"Silly boy," I said. "Be good."

She pulled out two treats and handed me the bag.

Potato wailed and rolled on the floor dramatically.

"He's giving you quite a show," I said with a laugh.

"Okay, okay. Here you go." She set the treats on the ground and he chomped them happily and then rubbed against her, purring again.

"He'll love you forever now." I pulled out the charcuterie tray from the fridge and took off the wrap on it. Still looked good.

"Oh, wow, that's really nice. You really didn't have to do this," she said, and I was a little bit embarrassed.

"Sorry. I guess it's a little much." I looked down at the tray and wanted to run away.

Esme took a few steps toward me and put her hand on my arm. "No, it's really great. I'm just not used to interacting with people outside of a bar." This was said with a laugh. "I don't get out much."

I found that hard to believe, but she said it with sincerity.

"Shall we take this to the porch?" I said, and then wanted to cringe at how formal I sounded.

"Sure," she said. It was an absolutely glorious afternoon. Not too hot, and the breeze was blowing just perfectly. Only a few wispy clouds dotted the sky that was so blue it almost hurt to look at.

"Oh, this is gorgeous, you're so lucky," Esme said, settling herself onto the couch. It was just big enough to accommodate two people, but my thigh brushed against hers as I joined her.

"It's not much, but it's mine." I didn't want to pry and ask her why she didn't have her own place, but I had to admit, I was curious.

"I know I've grown up here and I should be used to it, but I'm still always shocked at how beautiful this place is," she said.

A seagull flew overhead, and I heard the distant sound of a boat chugging through the water. Very faintly, voices drifted out the open windows of my neighbor's homes. Nearly all of them were occupied during the summer. In the winter things got much quieter. When so many people were around, I got annoyed, but in the winter, things could get bleak and lonely.

Esme sighed and leaned back on the couch. Her eyes skimmed the water, and I tried not to stare at her too much. I still couldn't believe she was in my house. Without taking her eyes off the ocean, she reached for a piece of cheese from the plate. I did the same, if only to give myself something to do other than gazing at her.

The silence between us wasn't awkward. I kept expecting it to turn and for me to feel strange and uncomfortable, but that feeling never came. We just sat there together, looking at the natural beauty in front of us and munching on snacks and sipping our drinks.

Esme sighed and set her empty drink can down. I blinked, unsure of how much time had passed since we'd been sitting here.

"I can't stop thinking about the idea of a silent retreat. It sounds amazing." she said, finally. We'd talked about her wanting a break from her life before. Sounded like she really needed it.

"My mom tried to get me to go on one of those, but I had so much anxiety about the no-talking that I refused to go," I admitted. "But I'm not a bartender who has to talk to people for hours on end. That sounds like it would wear on you after a while."

She nodded and slid a cracker between her lips. "I don't hate my job, I promise. It's just too much sometimes. I crave quiet. Like this." She gestured at the ocean. "I want to go out there and float and let all the thoughts drain from my head until there's nothing left."

I finished my drink, making sure to not let the ice fall on my face. "You know, they have those sensory deprivation tanks. There probably isn't one in Castleton, but I bet there's one in the state." I'd written a listicle for a website that mentioned them once. Like the silent retreat, it sounded like something that would give me a panic attack, but maybe it could help Esme.

"Huh. I've never heard of that. Thanks."

"Sure. I know lots of completely useless stuff. It's an occupational hazard of being a content writer." Esme pulled her legs up onto the couch and faced me.

"What other kinds of useless things do you know?" I willed my face not to get red at her increased attention.

"Hmm, let's see. I did a huge list of unusual date ideas for a dating app. Then there was the 'What is Your Cat Thinking?' article, and one of my favorites that was instead of your zodiac signs, you'd take a quiz and get assigned a different kind of plant. I was a daisy. Sweet, steady, and utilitarian. Something like that."

Esme laughed. "I wonder what I'd get. Probably a cactus or

something."

"No, definitely not. You're only prickly when you have to be. Maybe a rose with a few thorns on it."

Esme looked down and then tucked her hair behind her ear. "You're sweet."

Sweet enough to fuck, I hoped.

Potato screamed inside the house to come out and sit with us, so I let him out and he immediately tried to go for the plate of snacks. I handed it to Esme and pushed him away. "Go play with your toys, you dork. There is nothing on this plate you want." He yowled, but I found one of his toy mice on the floor and threw it to the other side of the room for him to chase.

"I should probably go," she said, putting the plate back down on the table. That was it? I didn't want her to leave.

"You don't have to. You can stay. I can even just, like, go in the house and you can chill here alone of you want." Anything to get her to stay. Hell, she could use me as a footstool if it would get her to stay.

"You don't have to do that, Paige." She got up and walked toward the door to go back through the house and out to her car.

"I have cake," I said, in a last-ditch effort. Like that was going to work.

She turned slowly and raised one eyebrow. "Cake?"

"Yeah. It's from Sweet's." There was always some form of cake in my house, whether in the fridge or the freezer. Having Linley as a best friend had many perks.

"What kind?" she asked.

"It's their classic double chocolate hazelnut cake. You're not allergic to nuts, are you?"

She shook her head slowly, a smile forming. "Nope. And chocolate is one of my main food groups."

"As it should be," I agreed. "Want some?"

She held up a finger. "One piece."

Chapter Eight

ONE PIECE of cake quickly became two.

"And then Batman had to climb on the bar to get him down so he didn't get arrested," she said, and I gasped with laughter, tears streaming down my face.

"I can't believe it," I said, wiping my eyes. "Who knew our mild-mannered math teacher loved Taylor Swift so much?"

"It was quite the impassioned speech. I'm sure someone caught it on their phone and it will somehow work its way onto the internet someday. *Man Really Loves Taylor Swift. Really.*"

"You've seen everything," I said, going for the last bite of cake on my plate. I hoped I didn't have any crumbs in my teeth. I loved hearing her bartender stories.

"Have you ever considered writing a book? You really should. Just change the names a little bit. Plus, most of the people were too wasted to remember anyway," I said.

She yawned and covered her mouth. "No, I wouldn't do that. It's against bartender-customer privilege." She set her empty plate down and sighed.

I snorted.

"Okay, *now* I really should go. You've given me enough of

your time and food for one afternoon." She stood, and this time I had no other tricks up my sleeve to get her to stay.

"It was my pleasure," I said, following her back through the house. She gave Potato lots of attention before straightening up and looking at me.

"Thank you so much for the flowers," I finally said.

She smiled, and my stomach flipped over. Twice. "Thank you for the cake and conversation. This has seriously been the best part of my week, Paige." I found that hard to believe, but I blushed anyway.

"That's really nice to hear. You're welcome anytime, right Potato?" I asked and he ignored me to stare up at Esme. "I think he's in love with you."

"The feeling is mutual," she said.

There was a pause that was thick with things unsaid.

"You can come back whenever, really," I said, to fill the silence.

She leaned forward. "I'd like that. Really."

"Good," I said on an exhale.

Esme leaned even closer and my heart pounded so loud that I was sure she could hear it. Was she going to kiss me?

I *wanted* her to kiss me. I wanted it desperately.

No! That wasn't how this was supposed to go! I was supposed to be the seducer. She was supposed to be desperate to kiss *me*.

She inhaled sharply and pulled back. No kiss.

"I'll see you later, Paige," she said, and I swore I heard a note of frustration in her voice.

"See you later," I said, hiding my trembling hands behind my back.

She got in her car and I watched her pull out of the driveway. I didn't shut the door until she'd turned the corner and disappeared. I leaned against the closed door and put a hand on my heart, hoping for it to stop beating so hard. If I was going to be in control of this situation, I had to be in control of myself.

So what if Esme almost kissed me? It wasn't a big deal. People almost kissed every day.

Get it together, Paige.

Next time I would take charge. Next time, I'd be in control, Next time, I'd be the seducer. I'd be mysterious and sexy and she wouldn't be able to resist me.

I had plans to make.

"SO WHY DIDN'T *you* kiss her?" Linley asked the next day, when I stopped by the bakery to give her an update on my afternoon with Esme.

"Because it wasn't the right time," I said.

"Why not?"

"Because!" I said, and then realized I was yelling. "Because I have a plan, and kissing is the next step, but I have to lure her some more first. Wyatt would have tried to kiss her. I'm being better than Wyatt."

"Okay, okay," she said. Currently she was rolling out pie crusts for the summer strawberry pie. I had already ordered one for myself and one for my mom when they were done, with a tub of fresh whipped cream that they made in huge fluffy batches. Sometimes I just ate that stuff with a spoon.

"I'll just have you know that my cake played a part in this plan, and I'm going to be smug about it," she said, pushing the rolling pin with practiced ease.

"Your smugness has been well-earned. You're welcome to it."

"Excellent."

She carefully lay the pie crust in the pan and then crimped

the edges before getting it back in the fridge and moving on to the next crust.

"Gray's taking me out this weekend. We're meeting in the middle again, but this time at a new place. I let him pick this time."

I leaned on the counter. "What are you wearing?"

"So, I was thinking about that cute dress I got when we went thrifting last month. You know, the yellow one with the flowers?"

"The one that's both pioneer and sexy at the same time?"

"Yeah. If it wasn't so hot, I'd wear it with my black boots, but I think sandals will be better."

I nodded in agreement.

"I'm packing condoms and lube in my purse. Just in case," she admitted, as if she was commenting on a change in the weather.

I cupped my hand around my ear. "Excuse me, Linley? Did I hear that right? You're bringing condoms and lube on your date?"

Her eyes went wide. "Shhhh, I don't want my parents to hear. They don't need to know about my sex life." She said the last part in a hushed voice.

"Well, you shouldn't have brought up condoms," I said just as Martha walked into the room.

"What about condoms?" She glared at me and then looked at Linley and back at me as I floundered.

"I was uhhh, just talking about them because people should use them. People who are having sex. Not me, obviously. I never have sex." I couldn't stop babbling and Martha's eyes just got more and more narrow as I flailed.

"Mom, I'll be done in ten," Linley said, saving me. Martha gave me one last look and then turned to her daughter.

"Condoms are important, not just for pregnancy prevention, but they also protect you from STDs. I want you girls to remember that." We each got a Mom Glare before she left the kitchen again. I almost collapsed on the floor.

"Your mom can be terrifying sometimes. Holy shit," I said.

Linley braced herself on the counter. "I am never talking about *that* in here again. Thanks for trying to save me."

"I'm not sure how much saving I did, but you're welcome anyway. What are friends for?"

ESME and I kept sporadically talking via text and voice memo for the rest of the week. I stayed away from the bar on purpose and tried not to talk to her *too* much. Had to leave her wanting more. She also had times when she was just unavailable, probably while she was at work, so I got used to not hearing from her for a while.

Esme had a biting wit that I hadn't known about until now. She didn't take a whole lot of things too seriously, and she loved her dad fiercely. She didn't talk about what happened to her mom, but it wasn't like everyone in town didn't know that she'd passed away from cancer when Esme was nine or ten. I couldn't relate to losing a parent like that, but my dad was gone from my life, so that part I could understand.

I sent her lots of videos and pictures of Potato, and even some of the fish. In return, she sent me voice memo jokes from the regulars at the bar, told me her best and grossest bartender stories, and cracked me up with tons of awful memes.

"Hey, so do you want to hang out again? I actually put my foot down and took Sunday off, if you can believe that. I'm trying to get better about not working so hard that I fall asleep in my car when I get home and then have to drag my ass to bed," she sent as a voice memo, a few nights after she'd come over. The roses she'd gotten me were still blooming beautifully on my counter.

Good for you. Setting boundaries is really good. It's something I'm constantly working on. I'd love to hang out. The weather's supposed to be nice. How about going to the beach?

I wasn't just suggesting going to the beach so that I could see her in a bathing suit. No, I also thought it would be fun to share a tray of French fries and maybe splash her in the water a bit. A fun, chill, sexy day.

"Hey, that sounds great. I honestly can't remember the last time I went to the beach. I'm not even sure where my swimsuit is." She laughed. "But I'll find it."

We agreed to meet each other in the morning at the beach, before the sun got too hot. I had a momentary image of Esme, wearing a vintage swimsuit and giant sunglasses, licking ketchup-covered fingers as she lounged on the sand. Hot.

I smugly told Linley and Em about my beach date with Esme, and Em asked if she could come over to my cottage for a wardrobe consultation.

"I mean, I want to help, but I also wanted to get the fuck out of my house. Wyatt keeps coming over with Gretchen and being gross, so I had to escape." She pretended to gag.

"Why is he coming over? He has his own place. That doesn't make any sense."

She flopped down on the couch. "This is what I'm saying. I think maybe he doesn't want to be alone with Gretchen because then he'd have to talk to her. Instead, he foists her on Mom, and Gretchen just does not know when to stop talking. I've never seen someone use that many words in my entire life."

She closed her eyes and lay back. "I need to move out."

"Then do it. I bet your parents would co-sign a lease for you. Just get out. Have the freedom to walk around naked."

Em opened one eye. "That does have appeal." She sighed

and sat up. "Okay, enough about me. Show me what we're working with in terms of beach wear."

I only had two suits that I really liked the way I looked in, and my cover-up was a simple white gauzy dress that made me feel like a mermaid or something when I had it on.

"Definitely this one," Em said, pointing to my white and black flower pattern suit. It was honestly the one that made my boobs look the best, so it was a clear winner. I laid it out on the bed with the cover over it to show the final look when I put it on.

"Love it," Em said. "If it wouldn't be totally weird, I'd ask if I could come."

"You know if I didn't have this seduction plan, I would totally invite you."

She waved a hand. "It's okay. I won't stand in the way of a good seduction."

I put my suit and cover-up on the top of my dresser. "You should have a seduction of your own." I raised my eyebrows up and down.

"Ugh, that seems like so much work. Why would I do that when I can just wallow in my loneliness while my brother noisily makes out with his girlfriend in the living room and my mom pretends to ignore it."

"Oh, gross. I'm glad he never did that with me." We'd done our fair share of making out, but never like that.

"Yeah, thanks for that. I appreciate it," she said.

I shoved the image of Wyatt and Gretchen sucking face out of my mind. I didn't need that poisoning my brain, thank you.

"I mean, I don't know. Maybe online dating or something. I doubt I'm going to find anyone here." It was true there weren't as many queer people in Castleton as, say, in a big city, but we had our fair share. I'd never had any problems, but Em had more sense and higher standards than I did. I was an adult enough to admit it.

She lay herself out on my bed on her back, her feet still on the floor. I laid out next to her on my side.

"Sorry, I'm being gloomy." She closed her eyes.

"Hey, it's okay. We all get gloomy sometimes. And don't worry. You're literally twenty-two, Em. You're not dead yet," I said.

She opened one eye and tilted her head to look at me. "Thanks. That's a good reminder. Sometimes I feel like I haven't done anything, and that means I'll never do anything."

Em wasn't crying, but she looked like she might.

"Hey, it's okay. None of us know what the fuck we're doing. Anyone who says they do is full of shit. We're all making things up as we go along. You're going to be fine. You're smart and hot and funny. If you want to change something, you have the power to do that." I cringed a little at my speech. "Sorry, I didn't mean to get all motivational speaker on you, but it's true."

"No, it was good, thanks. I needed to hear that."

I sat up and she followed me. I gave her a hug.

"If all else fails, I will help you come up with a new identity and you can flee to a fabulous foreign country and be someone else," I said.

"Now, that idea I like. I can have a tragic backstory that I tell. With just enough tragedy and mystery that I'm irresistible." She struck a pose with one hand on her head.

"See? You've got a backup plan," I said.

I WOKE with jitters on the morning of my beach day with Esme and I couldn't figure out why. It wasn't like this was a real date, in any sense of the word. Right? I would have known if it was a date. I mean, I'd planned the whole thing. This was *my* idea.

I checked myself in the mirror dozens of times before I said goodbye to Potato and grabbed my beach bag that had a towel, snacks, water, my portable phone charger, sunblock, and a bunch of other things in it.

I got out of my car and searched around for Esme in the packed lot. Not a single cloud dotted the sky, and it was due to hit nearly eighty degrees, which drove everyone out of their un-air-conditioned homes to find a bit of relief with the sea breeze and cool water.

Esme drove a rusty blue truck and I quickly found it in the lot. She got out and glanced around before spotting me and waving. I walked toward her on wobbly legs, only stumbling once, which was all I could really hope for.

"Thanks for thinking of this, I am in dire need of sand and sun," she said, smiling at me from under a massive black hat. Her sunglasses were black. Her one-piece suit was cut to like it came from the 1950s, and she'd covered it with a translucent black robe. Even her sandals were black. She looked so sexy, I couldn't even swallow.

"You ready?" she asked, after I was rendered speechless by her presence.

I unstuck my throat. "Yeah, I'm good. Let's go."

She put her tote bag on her shoulder and I realized it was one of the reusable canvas bags from her dad's store. Cute. It made her look less like a goth heiress. We paid at the ticket booth and walked down the wooden ramp toward the sand. Since we'd come relatively early, the sand wasn't completely covered by towels and other people.

"Where should we go?" she asked, looking left and right.

"Doesn't matter to me. I'm not picky." I was still too fluttery to function.

Esme walked toward the right side of the beach and I followed along behind her, trying not to fall in the sand as I tried to keep up.

"What do you think?" We'd had to go pretty far to find a clear area. I never liked to sit too close to anyone else. I liked my space.

"Looks good to me." There was at least a ten-foot radius in every direction. That was just about as good as it was going to get.

We set our things down and spread out towels. Esme's was black with little stars all over it. Mine had a picture of Potato on it. Linley had gotten it for me a few birthdays ago.

"I wish I brought a beach chair, but I haven't had one in years," she said, smoothing out the sand under her towel.

"Oh, sorry. I have two. I should have brought them." Shit. Why didn't I put them in the car? I hoped I hadn't ruined beach day already.

Esme touched my arm. "No, it's fine. Relax." The place she'd touched tingled even after she'd removed her hand and went back to fixing her towel. I did the same as she pulled her robe off, took off her hat, and beamed at me. There was so much skin to look at. So many horny thoughts in my head.

I didn't think I'd be doing much relaxing today.

The wind blew Esme's hair toward me, and it brushed against my arm. She twisted the strands together and put it behind her back before laying down and tilting her face up to the sun.

Whenever I went to the beach, I could never just lay there. Either I was listening to a podcast, or an audiobook, or reading something.

I tried copying her and closed my eyes for a few minutes, but then I heard Esme sit up probably less than a minute later. I opened my eyes.

She looked down at me. "Okay, so, I'm not really good at sitting still? I mean, I can watch a movie or read a book, but just sitting here is not working for me. Do you want to take a walk?"

It was as if she'd read my mind.

We got up and made our way down to where the water met the sand. The tide was coming in, so we didn't have to walk far to reach it. Esme stopped just out of reach of the waves.

I walked right into the water, going up to my ankles. "Come on, it's not bad. I promise."

I couldn't tell for sure, but I was sure her eyes narrowed behind her sunglasses.

"As long as you don't splash me," she said, and tiptoed toward the water as if it was going to bite her. The second her toes got the tiniest bit wet, she let out a banshee shriek that made people around us turn and stare.

"You liar, it's freezing!" She danced from foot to foot and kept making the most adorable little screaming noises. I laughed because it was such a cute and unexpected reaction from her.

"You get used to it," I said.

I held my hand out to her on a whim. She took it and joined me where the water was up to her ankles.

She huffed and puffed for a few seconds, but then she seemed to calm down. Her hand was still in mine. I hoped my palms weren't sweaty and my fingers weren't trembling.

She inhaled sharply through her nose. "Okay, I think I'm getting the hang of it," she said. I took a step further out and she came with me. Part of me expected her to drop my hand, but she didn't.

"Don't take me too far," she said, her grip on my hand nearly crushing my fingers. I wasn't going to let go.

"I won't," I said, squeezing her hand back. We kept holding hands, and I kept taking one step at a time until we were up to our waists.

"Okay, that's good," she said. "Are you ready to hear something extremely embarrassing?"

A bigger wave hit us and I wobbled a little on my feet, but

she kept me upright.

"Go for it," I said. "I won't tell anyone."

Esme leaned in toward me. "I can't swim."

I couldn't help it, I was shocked. I guess I assumed most kids who grew up in Castleton had learned at one point or another. We just had so much access to the ocean, as well as a small pond that was popular for swimming as well. My mom had enrolled me in a summer swim class when I was so young I couldn't even really remember learning.

"I was always too scared so I just never did. I'd put my feet in, but never really got all the way in the water. My great uncle drowned and I guess it always just kind of freaked me out. My dad tried to teach me, but I had a tantrum each time, so he stopped trying."

Her shoulders were up around her ears and I could tell she was really embarrassed. She didn't need to be. I had way more embarrassing secrets. Most of them involved bad sexual decisions. So much worse than not knowing how to swim.

"Hey, there're a ton of people who can't swim. I mean, unless you're going to be spending a ton of hours on a boat, why would you need it? It's not a big deal, Esme."

Her fingers stopped clenching on mine so intensely. "Thanks. I still feel weird about it. Every year I promise I'm going to learn, but I never end up doing it. Not very badass of me."

I stepped closer to her and swung our hands in and out of the water. "I still think you're a badass."

She looked down and smiled. "I appreciate that." She'd started shivering, so I suggested that we get out of the water and get moving to warm her back up.

"I was fine, but then I got really cold, I don't know why," she said as we stepped onto the sand again. Esme dropped my hand and I tried not to be upset about it. She leaned down and picked up a small rock, rubbing it with her fingers.

"What do you think?" she asked, holding it out to me.

"Maybe an owl?" I said, leaning in looking at the white spots on the darker gray stone.

"Oh, it does kind of look like an owl, you're right." She held onto the stone as we walked along. My hand was cold and empty.

Just ahead of us a group of kids ran into the water, screamed, and ran back out again, only to repeat the process over again. I remembered doing the exact same thing when I was younger. Or surfing on the waves with a boogie board.

"I can't believe I told you that I can't swim," Esme muttered.

I avoided stepping on a huge clump of seaweed. "Do you want me to share something embarrassing to make up for it?" I suggested.

That made her laugh. "I mean, only if you want to."

I searched my brain for something along the same lines. She didn't need to know any of my embarrassing sex stories. At least, not yet.

"So, I went on a date with this girl in college who was absolutely obsessed with Marie Antoinette. She didn't wear wigs or anything, but she always wore corset tops and ruffles and her dorm room was decorated like Versailles, if you can believe that. I have no idea what I was thinking, but she'd flirted with me and I agreed to grab a drink with her. We ended up back at her place in this bed that she'd tried to make into a canopy with this massive gold comforter and she wanted me to say 'let them eat cake' while we were having sex."

As soon as I started to tell the story, I realized this was the wrong story to tell, but it was too late and I couldn't back out, so I just… kept going. I finished and snuck a look at her. She had her mouth open.

"And you didn't go on a second date?" she said, in feigned shock.

"Sadly no. The sex was good, but not good enough to put up with the rest of her shenanigans. I pretty much ghosted her and we never saw each other again. I wonder whatever happened to her. I'm not sure if I want to know."

One of my strangest dates for sure. I still couldn't believe it had actually happened.

"I bet she's really boring now. Or she's in deeper than ever. It's one of the two extremes," Esme said.

"Exactly."

"In the spirit of sharing bad dates, how about I share one?" she said, and I almost tripped and fell. I knew next to nothing about her dating life. She kept it pretty quiet somehow.

"Do tell," I said.

Esme took a breath. "Okay, so, I met this guy online. He seemed cool, and after talking for a while, we agreed to meet at a coffee place. He'd clearly tinkered with his pictures, which, whatever. But then when we were talking I realized this was definitely not the same guy I'd been talking to online. I didn't know *who* he was, but he wasn't my date. So, I tested him and told him things that weren't true about me and he was all like 'oh yeah, right.' He was full of shit, but I wasn't sure how to confront him. I just kept drinking coffee and waiting for him to crack. It actually didn't take that long. He got a call on his phone and went completely red and then went outside to take it. I kept my eye on him, but after talking for a few minutes outside, he literally bolted. Ran away. Gone."

I literally wouldn't have believed this story if someone else had told me about it. Who the hell would run away from Esme? WHO?

"Wow," I said. "That's... wow."

"Exactly. So I sat there and tried not to cry and then I got up and went to order something to eat because I was starving after all that coffee and the baristas had figured out what happened so they gave me a bunch of free shit because they felt bad. And I got all their numbers so, who won in the end?"

She smirked at me.

Now *that* part I could believe.

We'd reached the end of the beach, so we turned and walked back the other way, talking about more bad dates. It wasn't hard to share things with Esme. I was also curious about her current dating practices, so I was hoping she'd open up about that.

"I don't know. Everyone acts like dating is supposed to be so fun and easy, but I'd just like to skip to arguing about the paint color on the kitchen cabinets instead. I want to be married," she said.

My heart thumped heavily in my chest.

"You can't really get to the marriage part without the dating part, unless you are willing to skip a bunch of steps. I mean, there are people who get married when they barely know each other, but that's not generally advisable," I said.

We both shuddered.

"Yeah, I don't think I want to do that," she agreed with a laugh.

Esme and I walked and walked until our suits dried and then we went back to our towels. The day grew hotter and I could feel my skin starting to crisp, so I did another layer of sunscreen and so did she.

"Do you want me to get your back?" she asked.

"Yeah, sure," I said, my voice squeaking. Why was I making such a big deal of this? I needed to calm down.

Esme took her time rubbing the lotion onto my back, making sure to move the straps of my suit so she didn't miss a spot. I sat there and tried not to freak out about the fact that she was touching me.

Too soon she said, "all done" in my ear and I turned my head to find her closer than I expected.

"Thanks."

She smiled and handed the sunblock bottle back. "Can you do me?"

Esme pulled her hair over her shoulder and presented me her back.

For a second, I forgot how to use my hands and dropped the sunblock before fumbling to pick it up at least three times. At last, I got it open and squirted some into my hand.

Esme's suit was a halter, so her upper back was completely exposed. Her flower tattoos flowed over her shoulder and went down her side. Otherwise, her back was free of ink. Just an expanse of beautiful skin that my fingers trembled to touch.

I started with the tattooed area, marveling at how bright the colors were.

"Your tattoos are pretty," I said. She looked at me over her shoulder.

"Thank you. I've had them for years, and I keep thinking about adding more, but I can never make up my mind." I moved my shaking hand faster, going across her upper back.

"I know what you mean. I keep thinking about getting one, but I'm so scared about hating it in a few years that I can't. What made you chose this?" Whew, at least that was a normal question.

She inhaled through her nose and didn't answer for a while. My hand slowed, working in circles. The sunblock was mostly rubbed in, but I didn't want to stop touching her.

"It's taken from a painting my grandmother did that hangs in my dad's house. Seemed fitting. I've always loved it, and I was itching to do *something* after a breakup."

Oh, I'd been there. After a particularly bad breakup I'd made an appointment to pierce my nipples but had caved at the last minute and had cancelled. After Wyatt, I'd also considered shaving my head. I'd even put clippers in my cart but then hadn't purchased them.

"It's really stunning," I said, and finally stopped touching her. I cleared my throat. "Do you want to have lunch?"

She looked back at me and our gazes locked for several seconds. Was she going to say something else?

"Sure. Let's go eat."

She got to her feet and held both hands out to help me up. We ended up closer than I intended and it took a few moments for her to drop my hands again before she picked up her cover-up. I put mine on as well, and we grabbed our wallets from our bags.

"You think our stuff will be okay?" she asked as we walked toward the snack bar.

"Yeah, it should be. Unless some seagulls run off with our towels. I once had one yank an entire hot dog out of my hand when I was a kid. I ended up chasing it down the beach, convinced I could catch it. No luck. I'm still sad about that hot dog." I pretended to pout.

"Aw, I'm sorry. Can I get you one to make up for it?" she said as we got in line.

"That might help. I'll probably need to get some ice cream too. And fries. Or onion rings. I can't decide."

"Let's get everything," she said, her eyes sparkling. Fuck, she looked so good. The wind kept tossing her hair around like a wind machine in a commercial and I couldn't stop staring.

We finally got to the order window and we did get just about everything. I covered my hot dog with ketchup and onions. Esme put relish and mustard and onions on hers. I made sure we had ketchup and ranch for the fries and onion rings. Somehow, we were able to secure a picnic table to ourselves and didn't have to share it with any random sticky children.

Esme bit into her hot dog and made a sound that was so sexy that I knew I turned red.

"This is so good," she said, after she'd swallowed. "I literally don't remember the last time I even had a hot dog."

I tasted my own, and it was delicious. The bun had been grilled with butter, which really put it over the top. We both finished our dogs quickly and moved on to the basket of fries and onion rings.

"I can't believe I have to go to work tomorrow," she said with a sigh as she picked up a fry and studied it.

"Why do you work so much?" Maybe that was too invasive, but it did seem like she worked a lot more than forty hours a week.

Esme munched the fry and thought about her answer.

"I guess I'm just used to it? I've been working a ton of hours for years, starting in high school. I mean, I was working weekends at the store for Dad when I was like eleven. He always worked a lot, so I guess I just did that." She lifted one shoulder. "I don't know. I need the money, for sure, but I guess I did it because I thought it's what everyone did."

She was right there. People in Castleton did work a lot of hours at multiple jobs. Teachers cleaned cottages in the summer, people drove plow trucks in the winter and mowed lawns in the summer, librarians worked weekends as waitresses. There weren't a whole lot of low-stress, low-hours jobs available, so people did what they could with their skills.

"No, that makes sense. I mean, if you *could* take more time off, you should. You have the rest of your life to work," I said.

I pulled out the biggest onion ring in the box.

"Holy crap, that is huge," Esme said.

"Split it?"

She nodded and I tore the onion ring in half and gave the bigger piece to her. Esme dipped it in ranch and ate it with satisfaction.

"I think I would take some more time off if I could have more days like this." She closed her eyes for a minute, as if she was savoring everything.

It was nice seeing her so relaxed. She was always so high-energy when she was working at the bar. Like she turned herself up to her highest level. Even her voice memos were kind of intense. Here at the beach she was... not subdued, just more at peace, I guess.

We finished all of our fried offerings.

"Now that we ate our lunch, we're allowed to have dessert," I said, before tossing the empty containers. Esme sucked down the rest of her soda and tossed the cup.

"We're very responsible adults," she said with a smile. "Our parents would be proud."

My mom wouldn't, but that was neither here nor there. I wanted ice cream.

Esme and I both ordered ice cream pops that were shaped like cartoon characters with gumballs for the eyes.

"I haven't had one of these since I was a kid," Esme said as she unwrapped hers. We'd moved to the shade and sat on the grass under a tree. I tried not to watch too much as she licked the frozen treat and I imaged her licking... other things.

She distracted me from thinking about that by pointing out the people walking by us.

"That's the second person riding a motorized cooler I've seen," she said, as a kid riding a blue rectangular cooler with wheels and what looked like a handle from a scooter on the front.

"That's not a bad way to get around. I might need to get me one of those. I'd probably put my laptop in there, though, in addition to snacks."

Esme sort of knew what I did for work, but I hadn't gone into a lot of detail, mostly because a lot of my job was really boring and just about answering emails.

"Oh, that dress is cute. I want to ask her where she got it," Esme said about a woman walking by. "She's pretty cute too."

Now I was really paying attention. The woman was probably about our age and had long flowing red hair and definitely had spent some time in the gym. I could see the definition of her quads from here as she walked by, a slit in her dress giving us a little peek.

"Yeah," I said, without thinking. I could feel Esme looking at me.

"So, what *is* your type?" she asked.

I almost dropped my ice cream.

"Uhhhh," I said as it dripped down my arm.

"You don't have to tell me," Esme said, after I struggled for a few seconds. "If you don't want to."

This was new territory and I had to be careful. I wiped the ice cream and got my thoughts together.

"I don't know what my type is? In the case of Wyatt, I think my type was 'people who will definitely hurt you, but you won't see it until too late', but that's not what you're asking. I guess..." I finished my ice cream and popped both of the gumballs in my mouth as I looked back at my dating history.

"I really go for people who are passionate. It doesn't matter what about. Someone could be into collecting workout videos from the eighties, but as long as it fires them up, I'll think they're attractive. Does that make sense?"

The gum lost its flavor after about a minute, but I kept chewing it, even after it turned into a more rubber-like substance.

Esme had been watching me the whole time and I was dying to know what she thought.

"That makes a lot of sense. I seem to be attracted to anyone emotionally unavailable or who cheats or who is secretly married and has a wife that lives in another state," she said.

I almost choked on my gum.

"That last one sounds extremely specific."

She gave me a look and popped the gum pieces in her mouth. "Do not recommend."

"Yikes."

She shrugged. "That's what I get for trying to date outside of Castleton, but it's nearly impossible to date someone from here, because of all the things I know. I can't date someone who's told me all their deepest, darkest secrets under the influence of too many tequila shots."

I wiped my sticky hands on the grass. "No, I totally get that," I said.

My stomach twisted in an uncomfortable way as I thought, *but what about me?*

I'd never gotten drunk and done any of those things. So, was this Esme's way of letting me down gently?

This had been a mistake. I'd miscalculated and my plan was blowing up in front of my face. She didn't want me.

My thoughts fired off in rapid succession.

Esme didn't want me.

Then she said, "but I'm thinking maybe I should change my type. You can do that, right? Change my type to kind people who listen to me bitch about my job and who give me the bigger half of an onion ring."

She stood up and dusted off her hands, as if she hadn't said much of anything.

I sat there looking up at her, wondering if she had actually said what I thought she'd said.

"Let's go check on our stuff," she said casually, but there was a hint of a smile on her lips.

"Yeah, sure," I said, and scrambled to get to my unsteady feet. I followed after her as we walked back down the ramp to the sand and I replayed her words in my mind.

I was completely and utterly confused.

ESME PULLED out her phone when we got back to our stuff and then flipped over onto her stomach.

"Do you mind if I go swim? I feel weird if I come here and don't do a few laps." I also needed to figure out where the hell to go from here.

"Sure, go ahead. I'll just read while you're gone. Just... don't get eaten by a shark," she said.

I laughed. "I think I'll be okay."

Sharks had been spotted at other beaches in Maine, but not recently and not at this one. I glanced back once at her as I made my way down to the water and dove in. She'd pulled a paperback out of her bag and was flipping through it.

It took me a lot less time to get in the water than when I'd had Esme with me. I dove right in. It was nice to focus just on my body and have no other thoughts as I adjusted to the cold and started moving my arms and legs.

There was a surprising amount of people in swimming, so I went out where it was deeper so I didn't have anyone in my path as I dipped my arms in and out of the water and kicked my legs and tried to breath as I got hit in the face by waves.

Once I got into the rhythm, my brain started thinking again. Esme had flirted with me. There was no way I was reading too much into what she'd said. She had specifically been talking about me. So, now I knew she was potentially open, and I could make my next move. It was honestly the best thing I could have hoped for.

I hadn't thought through what might have happened if she outright rejected me. Maybe I should have. I'd tried to go in with the confidence that I was going to succeed. My mom's self-help books had clearly left an impression on me when she'd read them to me while I was growing up.

Now that I had some sort of positive sign, I could go forward. It was time to go all in.

Chapter Nine

ESME WATCHED me as I got out of the water and I made myself walk slowly back toward my towel. I'd brought an extra one to use in case I went swimming, so I pulled it out of my bag as I shivered.

"Oh my god, your skin is all goosebumps," she said, brushing my arm. "Was it good?"

"Yeah," I said, still panting a little as I rubbed the saltwater from my skin and tried to wring it out of my hair a little bit.

"I think I'd rather try it in a pool first," she said with a laugh as I sat down, my towel around me like a cape. It would take a few minutes for my body to warm up again. A hot shower would be perfect right now, but I wasn't ready to go home yet. Laying in the sun for a few minutes would have to do the trick.

"If you ever want to go, I'd come with you. I mean, I'm not a professional or anything, but I could at least offer moral support," I said.

She shaded her eyes and then decided to put her hat back on. I did have one of those giant beach umbrellas somewhere. I should have thrown it in my trunk. Next time. I was hoping there would be a next time. A whole summer of beach days with Esme.

"When I'm ready I'll let you know," she said.

My phone rang and interrupted us. My mom.

"Hey," I said, looking at Esme and kind of sliding away from her on my towel. *Please don't let me fight with my mom in front of Esme.*

"Hi Sweetie, what are you up to today?" My eyes flicked to Esme, but she'd picked up her phone and had busied herself with scrolling through it.

"Nothing much. I'm just at the beach."

"Oh, by yourself?" There was a note in her voice that I didn't like. My mom wasn't a great liar, and I knew her well enough to know when she was fishing.

"No, I'm not alone," I said through gritted teeth.

"Interesting. Because Beth Carter-Bowerman said she saw you with Esme Bell looking *very* cozy at the snack bar." The smugness in her voice was so palpable, I was sure Esme could feel it.

"We're just hanging out. I'll call you later. Love you, bye!" I hung up before she could say anything else. She tried to call me back, but I put my phone on silent. Then she sent me a text message asking for more details.

"Everything okay?" Esme asked, looking at me from under the brim of her hat.

"Yup, just my mom, being my mom."

"Mmmm, I know what you mean. I have the feeling when I get home I'm going to get about a hundred questions from Dad because someone's going to go to the store and tell him that we were seen together." She pretended to gasp dramatically.

She was right. You couldn't sneeze in this town without someone whispering about it behind your back.

"I wonder if this is what it's like to be famous, having

everyone talking about your business. Only, famous people usually have a lot more money," I said, laying on my back and closing my eyes. I was suddenly completely exhausted.

"Hey," Esme said, and I tilted my head to look at her. "Want to make a sandcastle with me?"

I couldn't remember the last time I'd done that. It had been at least ten years or more.

"Sure," I said.

We decided that, in order to take this castle-building thing seriously, we needed tools, so Esme went to the rental shop and got us a full kit with different sized buckets, molds, and shovels.

"I don't know how people make those huge ones," I said, as my first few tries at pulling off the mold failed and the sand didn't hold the shape and just fell apart.

"The key is having sand that's moist enough, but also packed in tight enough," she said.

I made a face at her use of the word "moist."

"That's what she said," I responded.

Esme snorted a little laugh and my stomach did that little flippy thing like I was going down a hill on a roller coaster.

"So, what are you going to tell your mom about me?" she asked, as I tried to mix the right amount of sand with the right amount of water and push it into one of the molds that had little turrets in it.

"I haven't decided yet. Do you have any suggestions?" I asked.

Finally, I filled the mold and flipped it over in one smooth motion. We'd agreed before we started on a design.

"That depends on how much you want to tell her. You could just tell her you're hanging out with a friend. You could tell her you're just hanging out with me," she said.

Slowly, I pulled the mold off the section of wall. It came out perfectly.

"Is that what we're doing? Hanging out?" I asked.

Esme took the mold and started putting more sand in it, carefully tamping it down before adding more.

"For now," she said.

"For now," I repeated.

She gave me a little sideways smile. "The day isn't over yet. Anything could happen."

"IT'S BEAUTIFUL," I said, marveling at our finished sandcastle. We'd made it fancy with shell windows and a little rock pathway.

"Any crab would be happy to call it home," she agreed.

We both took pictures on our phones.

"And the waves will undo all our work, which is kind of beautiful. And maybe tomorrow someone will use these same grains of sand to make another castle," Esme said, rinsing her hands off in the bucket of ocean water I'd gotten earlier.

"Phew, I need to get out of the sun," she said, fanning herself.

"Same. I'm so toasted." I really felt like I needed a nap.

We walked back to our stuff and started gathering it together. My body was just a little sore from my swim earlier, which was satisfying. Plus, there was the whole "Esme is definitely interested" part. This day had been a success all around.

Esme and I dusted the sand off our feet as we stood near our cars.

"Thanks so much for this, Paige. It's been a really, really good day. I needed it," she said.

"I'm glad," I said, shuffling my feet back and forth in my sandals.

Be aggressive, Paige.

I had to make a move. I had to do *something*.

"I'll make you dinner," I blurted out. Wow. Brilliant. Why didn't I just go in for a kiss like a regular person?

"Dinner?" Esme said. She tapped her chin with one finger as if she was pondering that suggestion. "I'd love to have dinner with you."

Dinner could lead to dessert, which could lead to... other things. I was going for it. I'd gotten the green light. It was time.

Wyatt was going to be so pissed and it was going to be so great.

ESME AGREED to come over in a few hours, so I rushed home to shower, panic clean, and figure out what the hell I was going to make her that would impress her enough to fuck me.

Pizza. Most everyone liked pizza. There was a frozen crust in my freezer, and I found some fig jam and brie in the fridge, so we were going fancy. I also added some fresh arugula and herbs, caramelized some onions, and ripped up some prosciutto to add as well. I found a bottle of wine I didn't remember buying and pulled that out.

By the time Esme knocked on my door, the pizza was in the oven, and I had the coffee table all set up. I was pretty proud of myself for making such a classy meal that had actually been completely thrown together.

Potato ran to greet Esme as I yelled for her to come in from the kitchen. I'd also put on some music, hoping to really set the mood. I'd thought about candles but changed my mind at the last minute. Candles were a little *too* sexy.

I also made sure there were new sheets on the bed, and the pillows were in perfect arrangement. And that my lube was handy, just in case.

All systems were go.

"I think he loves you," I said, as Potato rolled onto his back for belly pets. He gave her complete heart eyes as he wiggled in satisfaction as she rubbed his belly floof.

"I adore him too," she said. "I figured since you have made me food twice, and it was your idea to go to the beach, the least I could do was bring appetizers and dessert." She held up two tote bags from her dad's store.

"Ohhh, I didn't think of dessert." Or appetizers. Oops.

"Hey, no worries. I know you made that beautiful charcuterie board, but I bought mine. And I didn't make this cake myself either." She pulled the containers out and set them on the counter.

"I won't hold it against you. Food is food." The cake went into the fridge, and I pulled off the top of the container.

"Now, we could plate this, or we could just go for it," I said.

"Go for it." She picked up a carrot and dipped it in the little container of hummus in the middle.

"The pizza should be done in just a few minutes," I said, and we took the board to the living room. Potato tried to attack it, but I pushed him away and then distracted him with a toy so he wouldn't bother us. He got bored with the toy and then fell asleep on the floor.

"I think I got a little toasted today," Esme said, pulling aside the shoulder of her t-shirt.

"Oh no," I said, looking at her reddened skin. "We should have paid more attention with the sunscreen. My mom was right."

"I remember Dad chasing me all over the yard with the bottle when I was a kid. I was so mad at the time, but now I want to thank him. Don't tell him that." She laughed at the last part.

"Yeah, I'm afraid if I told my mom she was right it would go to her head and she'd never let me forget I said that once," I said, dipping a floret of broccoli into the other creamy ranch dip included in the tray.

Esme sighed. "I know what you mean."

The timer for the oven went off and I retrieved the pizza.

"Oh my god, this looks so fucking good," Esme said, as I cut up the slices and then we loaded up our plates.

"I hope it is. I can't believe I even had prosciutto and brie at the same time. I am not normally this fancy, trust me." I picked up a slice and bit into it. The cheese was still a little too hot, so I burned my mouth, but whatever.

"Fuck, this is amazing," Esme said, her mouth full.

We were both silent for the next few minutes as we shoved as much pizza in our faces as we could without choking. It was a delicate balance.

"I should have made more," I said, when I realized we only had one piece left.

"Split it?" she asked.

"Always," I said. I ripped the piece in half, but she reached for the smaller one before I could give her the bigger one.

"You made the pizza. You get the bigger half," she said. For some reason, this made me blush and I tried to hide my face.

Esme took the dishes back into the kitchen and rinsed them in the sink before I could protest.

"I think I need to wait for dessert," she said, when she sat back down. I was nursing my second glass of wine, and hers was empty, so I poured her some more.

"Sorry the wine isn't better. I don't even know where it came from," I said. I also didn't know how to judge if wine was bad or good. I didn't drink enough to know the difference.

She took the glass from me. "No, it's fine. I don't know much about wine either. I watched this show about how even sommeliers can't actually tell the difference between expensive wine and cheap wine, so make of that what you will."

Interesting.

"I want to go on a vineyard tour sometime, though," I said. "I don't know, vineyards just seem so romantic."

Esme sipped her wine and leaned on the side of the couch so we faced each other.

"There's a vineyard about an hour from here," Esme said. "I'll go with you."

Oh.

"Okay," I said, my heart pounding louder than the music. "Would this be… a date?" Might as well figure that out now.

She set her glass down and leaned forward. "It is if you want it to be." Her voice got low and the air in the room thickened.

My skin got hot and I fought to keep my breathing normal.

"Yes," I squeaked. Why couldn't I talk in a normal tone when I got nervous around her?

"You wanna go on a date with me, Paige?" She smirked in that way that made my entire body tingle as if I'd been zapped by electricity.

I took a deep breath and willed myself to calm down. I was the seducer here. It was time to do a seduction.

"I want to do more than just go on a date with you, Esme," I said, with far more confidence than I felt.

I crawled toward her.

"Oh, you do?" she said, when our faces were only inches away.

"Mmmm, yes. So much more."

I gave myself one second of hesitation before I put one finger under her chin to tilt her head closer so I could kiss her. Her breath was sweet like the figs and her lips were so fucking warm and soft and it felt like it had been a thousand years since I'd kissed someone. My poor lips were starved.

Kissing Esme was… mind-blowing. A kiss was a seemingly simple thing: two sets of lips touching. This was *more*. So much more.

Her mouth moved with mine and, before I could take a breath, she slipped her tongue in my mouth and every plan I'd made dissolved and I forgot everything. Esme made a little satisfied sound in her throat and I somehow found myself pulled closer so I was basically laying on top of her. I couldn't wait a second longer to touch her hair, so I did, and it was so silky as it ran through my fingers and she kept kissing me, making my head spin.

"Ow," she said suddenly, and my eyes snapped open. "Sorry, hair." I let her sit up a little and she pulled the rest of her hair out from where it had gotten caught.

"Your hair is so beautiful," I said.

"Thank you."

I slid my fingers through the strands again. If she'd let me, I wanted to practice my braiding skills. Not right now, though. Later.

"What are you thinking about?" she asked.

"Braiding your hair," I said, before I could think of something better to say.

"You can braid my hair if you want. But I think you could put your hands to better use at the current moment."

I swallowed and this time, she was the one who kissed me and, once again, I was undone. Taking her suggestion, I left one hand in her hair and let the other do what it wanted. Tracing her cheek, feeling the pulse of her blood in her neck, fluttering along her collarbone.

Her fingers roamed up and down my back before sliding around my waist and then coming back up to cup my face. Esme's skin was so hot that I wondered if she was going to set me on fire. I felt like I was burning from the inside.

I sat up and before I lost my nerve, pulled my shirt over my head. I'd had enough time to find the prettiest dark burgundy lace bra I owned that I'd been saving for a special occasion. This seemed to qualify.

Potato attacked the shirt the second I tossed it on the floor.

"You're so beautiful," Esme said, looking up at me. "And I

would love for this to continue, but the skin on my back really hurts." I almost threw myself off her. She sat up with a wince.

"I'm sorry," I said, but I wasn't sure what exactly I was supposed to be sorry for. It was a reflex.

"It's not your fault, it's mine. I was a little too distracted to think about sunscreen," she said. I was about to say something else, but she took her shirt off and presented me her back.

"How bad is it?" she asked, and I looked at the angry, red expanse of her back that ended abruptly where her suit had been.

"It's not that bad, but it looks like it hurts. Hold on." I stood on unsteady legs and went to the bathroom, coming back with a huge bottle of aloe lotion.

"This should help. I have no idea why I bought this, but I'm glad I did."

Gently, I applied the aloe to her upper back.

"This, um, might be easier if you took off your bra. I don't want to get goo all over it." Said bra was black and simple, but oh, so sexy.

With one hand, she undid the clasp and slid the straps down her shoulders and freed her arms.

"That feels good," she said as I smeared more lotion on her skin.

"You should have said something earlier." I wouldn't have kissed her if I'd known she was suffering.

"And go back home without having kissed you? No way. It was worth it." She looked at me over her shoulder and it occurred to me that she was completely naked from the waist up.

No. I was helping her with a sunburn. The seduction was on momentary pause.

"Was it?" I asked, moving to her lower back. That part wasn't burned because it had been covered by her suit, but she couldn't see that. I'd take any excuse to keep touching her.

"Definitely. And I'm not going to let a little sunburn stop me from doing it again." The bottle almost slipped out of my hands. To be fair, the lotion had made my hands slippery.

Esme stood up from the couch and turned to face me.

Oh shit. Oh *shit*.

"Come on," she said, holding out her hand. As if we were in *her* house. But what was I going to do? I stood and followed her as she led me to my own bedroom.

"Leave the door open. If Potato can't get in, he'll scream outside the door," I said. She left the door partially open.

"I've wanted this for a long time," she said, leaning into me and speaking in my ear. Her nipples brushed against me and I stopped breathing.

"You… you have?" I asked. This was news to me.

"Yes. But you always seemed to be with someone else, and I thought I just wasn't your type." She fingered the strap of my bra.

"You're my type." She was *so* much my type.

"You're my type too."

The room was dark, but I wanted to see her, so I turned on the lamp next to the bed.

"You have a lot of pillows," Esme said, staring at my carefully made bed.

"How many pillows do you have?"

"A lot less than this. Where do you even sleep?" She laughed a little and I tossed the pillows I didn't normally use onto a chair.

"There. See?" I said.

Esme smiled at me. "Still seems excessive."

"Did you bring me in here to talk about pillows, or…" I asked.

"No," she said, undoing the button of her jeans and then sliding them down her legs. She wasn't wearing underwear.

Holy shit holy shit Esme Bell is naked in my bedroom.

"I don't think you want to talk about pillows either," she said, and lay on the bed, staring at me expectantly.

"No, I don't."

It took me a little more effort to get my own pants and underwear off before I joined her on the bed.

"Is this really happening?" I said, without meaning to.

"It is if you want it to be," she said, taking one finger and running it down my chest between my boobs.

"Yes," I said, and leaned over to kiss her.

So far, our kisses had been slow and sweet, but now that we were naked, we were both frenzied and frantic, touching everywhere at once for maximum skin contact.

We rolled over and over, gasping and reaching and touching and licking and tasting. Somehow I ended up on my back, and I wasn't upset about it.

Esme straddled my legs and kissed her way down my neck, every now and then leaving little bites that made me moan. Tomorrow I'd have marks and that turned me on even more. Let her mark me. I'd wear them with pride.

I arched my back as she took one of my nipples in her mouth, rolling her tongue around it and sucking. Her hair was everywhere, so I pushed it out of her face so I could see her. I had to see her face.

"Do you have a hair tie?" she asked, setting her chin on my stomach. I couldn't answer for a beat because she was just so sexy. Her ass was in the air, and there was another tattoo there that I hadn't had time to inspect yet.

"Oh, yeah," I said. Even though I'd cut my hair to my chin a few months ago, I still had some on my nightstand. I gave her one and she put her hair up in a sloppy bun before going back to torturing my nipples until I was begging and pleading. For what, I couldn't articulate.

"Fuck, this is so much better than I imagined," she said in a soft voice.

"You've thought about this?" I asked, as she kissed around my belly button.

"Many, many times."

That was news to me. Tonight was full of all kinds of revelations.

I wanted to say something else, but then she brushed my clit and I lost the ability to form sentences.

"Fuck, fuck, fuck," was all I could say as she kissed the insides of my thighs and let her clever fingers find out exactly how I liked to be touched.

Esme Bell had good instincts.

As if she was reading my mind, she thrust one and then two fingers inside me as she rubbed my clit with the heel of her hand.

Her mouth got in on the action and I came apart in a leg-shaking, breath-stealing, mind-blowing orgasm that snuck up on me so fast that I thought it was going to kill me as it burned through my body like wildfire. It ended gently, as I slid down the rest of the mountain and came to an exhausted rest back in my bed with a gorgeous woman between my legs. I didn't mean to come that fast. Oops?

"You going to make it?" she asked, as I panted and twitched in the aftermath.

"I'm not sure. Ask me in an hour." I said. I tried to touch her face, but my body was so limp that I couldn't raise either of my arms.

Esme smirked. "It takes you an hour to recover? Oh, what will I do with myself while I wait?" she said, sitting up and opening her legs so I could see all of her. As I watched, she licked her fingers and slid them down her stomach, moaning when she reached the right spot.

I was transfixed as she pleasured herself, throwing her head back and biting her lip and letting out the sweetest little moans. She was the most erotic thing I'd ever seen, and I didn't even think twice as I mirrored her actions, using my fingers on myself. I was already so wet from the previous orgasm and from her mouth that it was easy to slide three fingers inside myself, thrusting hard.

My sounds joined hers as we both brought ourselves closer and closer. I held back just enough so I didn't come before her, but I didn't know how long I could wait. If I was telling the truth, I was trying to have us come at the same time, but she went first, with loud cries and an arched back. Watching her threw me off for a second, but then I let myself fall as our noises blurred together.

"No fair," she said, looking down at me with hazy eyes. "You've already come twice."

"It's not my fault you decided to take matters into your own hand." I held mine up and wiggled my fingers so she'd get the joke.

She laughed low and leaned down to give me a kiss. "I couldn't help myself. Seeing you come turned me on so much that I couldn't take it anymore."

I kissed her back and then sat up.

"I think," I said, grabbing some bobby pins to hold the front of my hair back, "that it's your turn to catch up."

She touched her shoulder and winced. "One problem is that I don't particularly want to lay on my back right now. Still pretty tender."

I smiled, because that's exactly what I thought she was going to say. "Then it's a good thing I have all these pillows around, isn't it? Lay on your stomach."

It didn't take her long to figure out what I had in mind, and she lifted her hips so I could stack a few pillows and get her propped up at the right angle for what I had in mind.

In addition to getting an incredible view of her back, her ass was on perfect display.

I was so glad I'd turned the lights on.

"Is that a slice of watermelon?" I asked, looking at one of her tattoos on her left butt cheek.

"Yes," she said, and I could feel her trembling in anticipation. I kind of wanted to tease her a little bit.

"It's so cute. I wonder if it tastes as good as it looks," I said, brushing it with one finger, causing her to shiver.

She smiled at me over her shoulder. "Why don't you find out?"

I kissed the little tattoo and gave a her a little nip just to see what would happen. She made a noise and I looked up to check her reaction.

Her eyes were bright and hazy. "You can definitely do that again."

"Oh, really?" I chose another spot, and I was rewarded with a little moan. I left tiny bites all over her marvelous ass and she started grinding herself against the stack of pillows.

"Please, Paige. I *need* you," she begged.

I fluttered my fingers over her clit, just barely, and she was so responsive that I tried again. She pushed back, reaching for more.

"Please," she said.

I put my other hand on her back to make her be still.

"Patience," I said. "I'll give you what you want, I promise."

So I did.

I circled her clit with my fingers before slipping inside and fucking her that way. It took a little arranging, but I spread her legs wider and used my mouth as well. She pushed her hips against me as I thrust inside her with my fingers and sucked on her with my tongue and let her fuck herself against me until she came on my face and my fingers and I couldn't breathe, but I didn't care. She could use me however she wanted.

I didn't move until I'd felt the last of the little pulses squeezing my fingers subside.

She said something, but my ears were still in between her legs, so I lifted my head.

"What?" I asked.

"I can't believe we didn't do this sooner." Our eyes locked and I knew my face was a complete mess, but I didn't care. She was so fucking sweet, I couldn't wait to taste her again.

"We're here now," I said. "So let's make the most of it."

ALL TOO SOON, Potato made his presence known because his bowl was empty, and I also needed to feed the fish. I threw on a robe and let Esme use my extra one while I puttered around the kitchen and fed the cat and grabbed us some more drinks and a few snacks. I had no intention of sleeping tonight, so I was going to need some fuel to keep up my energy.

Esme let her hair down and combed through it with her fingers. It looked pretty tangled.

"What?" she asked, when she caught me staring.

"You totally have sex hair."

She raised her eyebrows. "And whose fault is that?"

I put my hand up. "Mine, definitely."

She laughed as I threw some crackers on a plate and then added the rest of the little snack tray she'd brought earlier that I had luckily put in the fridge. We went back to the living room for a little while and ended up talking about underrated bands, our favorite sandwiches, how we'd both like to travel to Iceland, and the most overrated movie franchises.

We twisted our bodies together, cuddling as I watched the way her mouth moved when she spoke and the way her eyes lit up when she got passionate about something.

What a knockout.

I still couldn't believe she was here with me, and I didn't want to take any second for granted, so I kissed her and that led to us shedding our robes and going back to the bedroom for more fucking. Her sunburn limited us a bit, but there were so many other things we could do, and we took full advantage.

A few hours later, we were both completely drenched in sweat, so we headed for the shower.

"I'm sorry, but I'm not using that," she said when I tried to hand her my shampoo to use.

"Why not?" I got really nice shampoo from her dad's store. It didn't have any chemicals or crap in it.

Esme held onto her hair with both hands, as if to protect it. "Because my hair is special and if I knew I was going to be staying over, I would have brought my stuff." She didn't even seem apologetic.

"Wow, rude. I'm insulted on behalf of my shampoo. It smells like coconut, see?" I opened the bottle and held it out to her and she winced away.

"No! Keep your inferior product away from my precious hair!" She couldn't exactly run away from me, but she shrank to the farthest corner of the shower, putting her hands up as if to protect herself.

"Now if I was really a bitch, I could so easily pop this top and you would have no escape," I said, shaking the bottle a little.

"Don't you dare, Paige!"

"But lucky for you, I'm not a bitch, so." I squeezed some shampoo into my hair and then put the bottle back on the shelf, turning my back to her.

"In that case," she said, pressing herself up against me, "I think you deserve a little reward."

I'd messed with her hair earlier, but this time she put her fingers in mine, massaging my scalp and working the shampoo through my roots.

"Oh, that feels really nice," I said, closing my eyes and relaxing into her touch. I didn't want to step under the spray and wash the shampoo out, but soon enough she grabbed the bottle of conditioner, making a face as she opened the top.

"I'm going to give you some of my stuff. It will change your hair." I wasn't paying attention to what she said as she worked the product through my hair.

"Mmmm," I said.

"Does that mean yes?" she asked.

"Mmmmm," I said again.

"I like that sound," she said in my ear, pressing up against me again, pushing me until my front was up against the shower wall.

"I'd like to hear you make that sound again. And again." She punctuated her words by sneaking her hand between my legs and stroking me.

"I can't come again," I said, pressing my hands against the shower wall, looking for something to hold onto.

"Not with that attitude you can't," she said with a little laugh. "You just need to believe in yourself, Paige. Believe in your... self..."

It didn't seem possible, but with a few twists and thrusts of her fingers, she had me on the edge again and I was a shaking, whimpering mess, completely at her mercy.

"Good girl," she said in my ear, and I wasn't sure if it was her words or a particularly deft thrust, but I shattered against her and she held me as I rode through the storm she was responsible for creating.

"I think your hair has been properly conditioned by now," she said, and I turned around to face her, completely boneless.

"That was mean," I said.

"Sorry not sorry," she said, kissing me.

~

IT WAS OBSCENELY LATE by the time we made it out of the shower, and we were both exhausted, so I didn't even ask if Esme wanted to stay the night. I just handed her a tank and some shorts and turned down the bed. The pillows we'd used to prop ourselves up were going to need to be washed, but I'd handle that at another time. For now, they all lay on the floor together. Casualties sacrificed in the name of fucking.

"Thanks," Esme said as she put on my clothes. It was strange seeing her wearing something of mine.

"You're welcome. You can wear anything of mine you want," I said.

She stepped closer to me.

"I don't mean just for the clothes. For tonight. And today." She kissed me so softly that I almost melted into the floor.

"You're welcome," I said, when she pulled back. "You're welcome for everything."

Chapter Ten

I WOKE to hair in my face and a cat meowing in my ear. Disoriented, I opened my eyes and remembered that I wasn't alone in bed, and not just because Potato was standing on me.

"Hush, Potato. You're fine." It couldn't be *that* late. I scrabbled for my phone and then squinted at the time.

"Oh, shit," I said, sitting up and dislodging an extremely grumpy cat.

"What?" Esme asked, blinking at me. Well, I thought she was blinking at me, but I couldn't see her through a veil of hair.

"It's eleven. I can't believe we slept in so late." I rubbed my eyes. In spite of actually sleeping, I didn't feel that rested. I *did* feel tingly and sore, like I'd been completely and fully worked over, so no complaints.

"I don't go in until four," she said. "So, I'm good. Did you have something due?"

I mean, I always had something due, but nothing that couldn't wait a few hours until I'd gotten myself together. Or at least had some breakfast.

I lay back on the pillows and started petting Potato.

"Are you hungry?" I asked. "I can make some eggs or something." I hadn't planned on making her breakfast, so I hoped I did actually have some eggs. If all else failed, I had some pastries from Sweet's in the freezer that I could bake in the oven.

"No, you don't have to. You've already done so much. I should get home." She made a face at the prospect. "At least Dad is at the store so I won't have to answer invasive questions about where I was and what I was doing."

Esme stood up and stretched her arms over her head, showing me a sliver of her belly.

"Does he do that?" I asked, watching her as she used one of my brushes on her hair, starting at the ends and working her way up. Her deft fingers wove a quick braid that she secured with the hair tie she'd used last night. I was never going to look at those things the same way again. For the rest of my life, I'd imagine the incredible girl with the tattoos pulling her hair back with one before putting her mouth on me.

Esme changed out of my clothes and put hers back on, and I had to sit on my hands so I didn't grab her and pull her back into bed.

"Do you ever wear underwear?" I asked, as she covered her perfect ass with dark denim.

She gave me a wink. "Sometimes. But never with these jeans. And never with certain kinds of pants."

This was information that I would ponder later, for many hours.

"Anything else you want to know?" She asked, looking at me as I lay in bed watching her.

"I think I'd like to know pretty much everything about you, Esme," I said. Potato curled into the warm blankets that Esme had vacated. He might be thrilled to see her gone from my bed, but I wasn't.

She walked over to my side of the bed and leaned down to

give me a kiss. I had morning breath, but she didn't seem to notice or care.

"It would take me a really long time to tell you everything," she said.

"I've got time," I replied, as she moved toward the door.

We'd spent nearly twenty-four hours together and all I could think about was when I was going to see her again.

"Maybe I'll come by the bar tonight and you can tell me a few," I said.

She leaned in the doorway. "Am I the only one who's required to spill their guts, or is this going to be a fair trade?"

"I'll show you mine if you show me yours," I said, and she made a little groaning noise.

"We did that last night and I'll be thinking about it for the rest of the day."

"Me too."

She gave me one last look. "Bye, Paige."

"See you later."

NORMALLY ALL I needed to focus on work was plenty of caffeine, a good to-do list, and a bustling café.

Nothing was working today. I'd been editing the same post for almost an hour, and I still had no idea what it was even about, and I wrote it.

It was only when Esme left that I remembered why I'd wanted to get her over and spend the night in the first place: to get back at Wyatt. My entire purpose for going after her was revenge and somehow... I'd completely forgotten until this morning.

Over and over, I replayed moments from the night. Esme, her head thrown back as she came. Esme, smiling at me as if I was the most delicious thing she'd ever tasted. Esme, laughing as we got tangled up in one another.

Esme, Esme, Esme.

She'd obliterated all of my carefully made plans. My beautiful plans, that were nothing in the face of a beautiful girl.

I was fucked, in more ways than one.

There were three options, as far as I was concerned. One, I could ignore Esme and attempt to ghost her in a town so small we didn't even have a traffic light. Two, I could go see her at the bar tonight and see what happened and keep my plans to myself. Or three, I could come clean, get my revenge, and ruin everything.

It didn't take me more than a few seconds of thinking to discard the first option. There was no way to pretend that last night didn't mean anything to me. I wasn't that good of an actor, that was for sure, and I'd have to come up with a hell of a story for why things had changed since this morning. No, ghosting wasn't going to work.

The third option... I still cherished the idea of telling Wyatt, in front of everyone, that Esme and I had fucked and I'd made her come and he never would. He'd get that throbby forehead vein, and his face would get red and it would be glorious. And every time I saw him from that moment forward, I would remind him of it, and rub it in his face. For the rest of our lives. I didn't think either of us was getting out of this town, so chances of seeing each other at least a few times a week were high.

Sweet. It would be so sweet and satisfying. As satisfying as finding a piece of the most delicious cake you didn't know you had and savoring every bite.

There was only one thing stronger than my desire for that slice of revenge cake, and that was my fear of hurting Esme. What would she think of me? I would never be able to face her again.

Why couldn't Wyatt have been obsessed with a girl from another town? Someone I could have had a no-strings fling with and never seen again?

No, it *had* to be Esme.

I'd picked the wrong girl. He'd picked the wrong girl.

If I could go back, I know what I should have done. I should have left her alone. Found some other way to get back at Wyatt. Now, I'd crossed a line I couldn't uncross.

There really was only one choice: I was going to forget about Wyatt and Esme was never going to find out what I'd done.

I DID my best to get through as much work as I could, but it was a relief when there was a tap on my shoulder and then Em appeared in my line of sight and waved. I took out my earbuds and she sat down at the table.

She had her "insurance clothes" on, as she liked to call them. I loved how glamorous she looked, but I also wouldn't want to have to wear fancy clothes every day. One of the benefits of being a freelancer was that I got to decide exactly what style mood I was in.

"Shouldn't you be at work?" I asked, and then I realized it was after five.

"Did you lose track of time? I don't want to be a jerk, but you look like hell." I probably did. It wasn't my fault that I hadn't gotten much sleep.

"I had a late night," I said, looking down at my computer and pretending to squint at an email.

"Uh huh. That doesn't have anything to do with the fact that Esme Bell spent the night?" I looked up in horror and then shushed her, afraid someone might overhear.

She gave me a puzzled look. "Why are you being weird? I thought that was your whole plan?"

I leaned back in my chair and rubbed my eyes. "It's complicated."

"Is it now?" Em crossed her arms and smirked at me. "Complicated how?"

I didn't answer.

"Paige. Complicated how?" Her eyes narrowed and I knew she knew. See? I couldn't lie.

"It happened. She came over last night and she left this morning." I shrugged one shoulder.

"Wait, I'm confused. Isn't that exactly what you wanted to happen? That was the whole plan."

I sighed and closed my eyes. I needed more coffee.

"Yes, but that was before it happened. Now everything is…" I waved my hands in the air.

"Ohhhhh. Seems like things didn't turn out the way you thought."

I closed my laptop. No more work was getting done today.

"No, it didn't, and now I have no idea what to do."

Em stood up.

"Come on. Let me buy you a latte and then we can figure this out."

TWO HOURS later I was at home with not only Em, but she'd called in Linley to assist.

"You really didn't need to do this," I said, when Linley showed up with broccoli cheese soup, bread bowls, and a jug of strawberry lemonade.

"I know, but what are friends for?"

It had been ages since the three of us had hung out.

"I told her I was going to see her tonight," I said, as Linley set up the food for us.

"Well, you're going to have to message her and say that something came up, because you need to figure out what you're going to do before you see her again," Em said, handing out spoons.

I looked at my phone and opened a new message to send to Esme.

Hey, so I probably won't see you tonight. Someone kept me up late and I'm behind on work. Talk soon?

She sent me a voice memo about ten minutes later.

"No worries, it's actually packed here tonight with live music and a bachelorette party, so I wouldn't have had much attention for you anyway. We'll talk tomorrow." There was a ton of background noise and I could barely hear her, but the tension in her voice was palpable. I guess it worked out in the end anyway.

"Okay, that's done," I said.

We all parked ourselves on the couch with our food and started strategizing.

"Don't tell her," Em said. "Put yourself in her place. How would you feel if she said that to you?"

Like shit. I would feel like shit.

"I've made such a big mistake," I said with a groan. "Why didn't you stop me?"

Linley pointed at herself. "I tried to and you didn't listen to me! I knew this was going to happen."

I scoffed. "You didn't know this was going to happen. You didn't think I could even get her to come over in the first place."

No respect for my seduction skills.

"Paige, it was a bad idea, and now you're in a situation. I hate to say I agree with Em, but I agree with Em. Telling her is only going to hurt her, and wasn't the whole goal to get back at Wyatt?"

"It was." Before. Before we'd gone to the beach. Before we'd built a sandcastle together. Before we sat together on the couch and ate pizza. Before we'd rolled around naked in my bed.

As much as I hated the position I was in, I didn't think I'd want to go back.

"What are you going to do now?" Em asked.

I ripped off a piece of the bread bowl and chewed on it.

"I'm not going to tell her. I can't. And I'm not going to tell Wyatt either. As much as I still hate that smug bastard, I'd feel worse about hurting Esme. So I guess that's that. My brilliant plan has officially blown up in my face."

I held up my glass.

"Cheers to Paige's failure!" Em said, and we all clinked our cups together.

"Another one for the books." I cringed at myself. "I'm really bad at this. You need to stop letting me plan shit from here on out."

Em raised her hand. "Can I plan your life from now on?"

"I don't think so. That would be giving you too much power."

"I could handle it."

Linley and I shared a look.

"Definitely not," I said.

Now that I'd made a decision about Esme, some of the weight lifted off my shoulders. I was more than happy to shift the topic from my disaster plan to Linley's new relationship.

"My mom is already asking when he's coming over for family dinner," Linley said. "If this doesn't work out, I think she's going to be more upset than me."

"How does he feel about your mom?" I asked. We'd moved

on to mixing the strawberry lemonade with wine to make a weird sangria-like thing that was totally delicious.

I was still totally exhausted, but it was good to have my friends with me. Everything last night had felt so surreal.

"He's probably carving her a set of birds right now," Emerald said with a laugh. Linley's mom collected all kinds of bird items including ceramic figures, paintings, plates. I never have to think about what to get her for any holiday. I already had a stockpile of bird puzzles that I'd saved up to give her next Christmas.

"He said he's open to meeting her, but that's only because he hasn't met her yet," she said with a laugh. "She's trying to send me on my next date with a basket of baked goods. I told her I'm not doing that, but I think she's going to break into my car and hide bread in the console." I wouldn't put it past her. That woman was intent on grandchildren, and she would stop at nothing to make them happen.

"You should just let her. It's cute," I said.

"It's all cute until she has the scones blessed or puts a spell on the pies or something." Oh, she would totally do that.

"But you like him, right?" Em said. "So, what's the problem?"

Linley rubbed the bridge of her nose and poured more wine into her glass, diluting any remaining lemonade.

"Because I don't want her to like him too much. And I don't want to get her hopes up. And it's weird!"

She had that right.

"I get it," I said. "I really do." My own mom wasn't the queen of boundaries either.

"Well, now that you two have shit going on, I'm feeling left out. Can we find me a fuck?" Em asked with a pout.

"I mean, fucks are plentiful, but is that what you want?" Linley asked.

Em thought about that. "I guess not. I've never really been

a fucky kind of person anyway." That was true. She'd always been far more serious and committed about her relationships. I'd even been with her when she'd turned down a fling and made vague excuses.

"What are you looking for?" Linley asked.

Em blew out a breath and looked at the ceiling. "I have no idea."

"How about we start with what you don't want?" I suggested.

"That's a good idea," Linley said.

The night devolved into making an extremely long list of all the things that Em did not want in a potential girlfriend. This included anyone who enjoyed reading Ayn Rand or played tennis.

"What's wrong with tennis?" I asked.

"I can't date someone who likes tennis," she said, but didn't elaborate.

"Okay, no tennis is on the list," Linley said. It was her idea to make an actual list on Em's phone of said qualities she did not want.

The list got more and more ridiculous as the night wore on until we were extremely tipsy and laughing about literally anything.

At some point the fact that I'd gotten barely any sleep the night before caught up with me and I felt my eyes starting to close.

"Okay, I have to work tomorrow, and so do both of you," Linley said. "And I have to work a lot earlier than either of you." She winced when she looked at the clock on her phone.

"You really need to have a talk with your boss," I said, as she got up and brought her glass into the kitchen.

"I know, but she's also my mom and she doesn't listen. If things get serious with Gray, I'm hoping to see if that will nudge her into letting me take some more time off. I can't be working on making grandbabies if I'm too exhausted from working in the bakery."

I gave her a hug. "That's brilliant and I love it. Thank you for coming over and not mocking me too much for my terrible decision-making skills."

I didn't need to ask either of them to keep my secret. I knew they would, as I kept their secrets.

"You're welcome. I'm always here for you, you know that." Linley and Em exchanged hugs as well and left me alone with a snoozing cat on the couch.

I was almost too tired to walk to my bedroom and get into bed, but somehow I managed and I was asleep instantly.

In the morning when my alarm went off and I saw that I was in bed alone (with the exception of the cat again), I couldn't help but be disappointed.

THE NEXT DAY I got myself back on track with work. I'd recently signed a contract to do transcription for a new podcast, so I was still learning the ropes for that. I was extremely close to overscheduling myself, and I was going to have to start saying no to things.

I was so engrossed in work that I missed a few text messages that I didn't check until I was taking a break for a caffeine refuel. Blue had made me a special drink today. They were always experimenting and I often agreed to be a guinea pig. Sometimes it worked out, and sometimes it went very wrong. Today, my drink tasted like a cake and a s'more and cheesecake all at the same time and I was going to have to ask how they'd made it because I definitely wanted to order it again.

I sucked down the last of the drink from around the melting ice cubes and went through my messages. One from my mom, asking when I was coming over for dinner next. I'd probably have to do that this weekend. One from Em, which was a silly meme, and one from Esme.

You up for a free drink tonight? I'd love to see you.

I wanted to see her too, but I was a little worried about how to pretend like everything was normal.

Sounds great! See you around 8?

She wrote back that sounded good and I tried not to panic.

I had to get my shit together, and get it together convincingly.

I'D CONSIDERED TELLING my freelance group chat about my predicament, but I didn't think I needed any other opinions on what to do. The whole thing was also so embarrassing that I didn't really want them to know about it.

I finished my workday, went home and had dinner, put on a cute outfit, and headed to the bar.

Of course, the first person I saw wasn't Esme. It was Gretchen, leaning against Wyatt and throwing her head back in a laugh, as if she was acting in a movie or a music video.

So. Fake.

I looked away as quickly as I could, but she spotted me and then whispered in Wyatt's ear. He flicked his eyes in my direction and then said something to Gretchen that made her howl as if he was the funniest person on the planet. Having had extensive experience with his humor, I knew he wasn't.

Trying not to shrink back, I lifted my chin and headed right for the bar. There was only one empty stool. Thirsty Thursday was in full swing, and the place was so boisterous that I couldn't hear myself think.

Esme was going at max speed, swiping credit cards,

pouring beers, and mixing rum and Cokes with remarkable grace and efficiency.

She smiled at everyone, but when she saw me, her eyes crinkled in a way that they didn't when she was looking at the person who'd ordered a drink before me. A little warm rush of satisfaction flowed through me.

"Hey, I was hoping to see you. Give me two seconds." She held up two fingers and I nodded. She was clearly swamped because I didn't see anyone helping her. Hopefully Batman was just on a break because there was no way she could serve all these people on her own without collapsing.

She came back a few minutes later and plunked a drink in front of me.

"Let me know what you think."

I didn't have the chance to ask what was in it before I heard a voice asking if Esme could make her drink again, "this time with DIET Coke." Emphasis on the second to last word.

I didn't turn around to confirm who the drink returner was because I didn't have to. I knew Gretchen's voice, even in a loud and crowded bar.

"Sure, no problem," Esme said, dumping out the cup and getting another to make the drink.

Gretchen let out a little sigh like it was taking too long, and I tried not to say anything. I didn't know what she was doing, but her presence was a constant irritation.

Esme handed the new drink over.

"With lime," Gretchen said without taking it. Esme added a lime wedge to the side of the glass.

"Finally," Gretchen said, and took it without thanking Esme, who smiled until Gretchen's back was turned and then rolled her eyes.

"Listen, I'm friends with her boyfriend's sister, and I can get dirt on her if you want," I said.

"Tempting, but she's nothing special. I've made hundreds

of drinks for cranky people. I won't even remember her by the end of the night." I hated that that was true. She didn't deserve to be treated like shit. No one did.

"Let me know if you ever change your mind." I sipped my drink and was hit by a sweet and smoky kick at the same time, and I wasn't sure if I liked it, even after I swallowed.

"No good?" Esme asked, watching me.

"I don't know?" I said truthfully. I took another sip and let the liquid sit on my tongue. It was like nothing I'd ever had before, but I decided after my second sip that I did like it.

"Good. No, definitely good." By my third sip, I was convinced.

"Sometimes drinks have to grow on you," she said, leaning forward.

"True," I said. "That's true of a lot of things. Songs, people."

She leaned even more forward.

"I don't think Gretchen is ever going to grow on me," she said.

I shuddered.

"Same. Sometimes your initial impressions of people are correct," I said.

She smiled and then was called away again.

I savored my drink and watched her work. Batman came back, at last, and helped, but it was still a really busy night. I ended up having a chat with a local guy who wouldn't stop telling me about how much he missed his ex-wife, and then switched to talking about his daughter and her dog breeding business.

I let him yammer on because he was sweet, but I also kept a fraction of my attention on Gretchen and Wyatt, who had been joined by friends. Townies that I didn't hang out with. The group got progressively louder as they drank more, and it grated on me.

They had every right to be here, but their energy was so annoying, and it wasn't just because I couldn't stand Wyatt.

I remembered being the girl on his arm, the one who had to listen to the same stories week after week and pretend to be interested. That wasn't even getting into the gross comments and borderline bullshit they said without even thinking. I'd felt like I needed a shower every time to wash off the interactions when I'd come home.

I was grateful I didn't have to do *that* anymore, although I could have done without the horribly broken heart.

My drinking companion found another friend to tell his stories to, so I finished my drink while scrolling my phone and occasionally glancing up at the TV, which had a sports channel on, naturally.

"How's it going, Cupcake?" a voice said in my ear, and I almost fell off my seat, but I was too closely packed in with people on either side so that wasn't going to happen.

I didn't respond to Wyatt, so he tapped me on the shoulder, and I had no choice but to turn around and give him my attention. At least, until I could make him go away. He was not driving me out of this bar.

"You seem pretty cozy with the bartender," he said with a smirk. Once upon a time, his smile made me weak at the knees. Now it only made me want to punch him in his smug face.

"I don't know what you're talking about," I said, in what I hoped was a mild tone. I couldn't let him rile me up. Not here. Not where Esme could see. I didn't want her to know how much it still cut me to see him all the time. How much it hurt to see him sticking his tongue down someone else's throat, and whisper in someone else's ear.

"She'd never go for you. She's just hoping to flirt with you for tips," he said, and I could tell how confident he was in this assertion. Wrong, but extremely confident, which was how he generally went through life.

It took everything in me not to tell him how wrong he was. How that I'd not only seen her completely naked, but I'd made her come last night. Eight times.

But if I told him, then she was going to find out the only reason I'd asked her to stay over was to brag about it, and the thought of her finding out made me feel sick inside.

So I pressed my lips together and didn't respond to Wyatt's obvious baiting.

"How are things going with Gretchen?" I said instead, changing the subject.

He leaned forward, as if he was sharing a secret. There was nowhere for me to go, so my back pressed against the wood of the bar, digging into my spine. He'd invaded my space and I couldn't escape. Typical Wyatt.

"Let's just say that Gretchen is very good at being *very* bad. Unlike some people. She's not uptight about expressing herself."

This was a dig directly at me and he knew it. Wyatt was great at giving orgasms, but he'd also been into some things that I hadn't, and I'd let him know it wasn't going to happen. He used that refusal to call me a prude. I hadn't seen it at the time, but it was seriously shitty behavior, and thinking back on it made me want to give him a good dick kick.

"How nice for you," I said. "Gretchen is so blessed for having you as a sex partner."

Why wouldn't he just go away and leave me alone?

The urge to blurt out that I'd done some fucking of my own was strong, but I was not going to throw Esme under the bus.

"Too bad you missed your chance," he said, and gave me the slimiest smile.

I was about to say something, anything, when my drinking companion jabbed Wyatt with his elbow.

"Why don't you leave the lady alone? I don't think she's

interested." His voice was full of gravel and cigarette smoke, and his flannel shirt was probably older than I was.

"What?" Wyatt said, turning to speak to this intruder.

"Move along," the guy said, jerking his thumb in a 'go away' motion.

Wyatt glared, but turned around and walked away, going back and giving Gretchen a long kiss, tongues in full view as he simultaneously grabbed her ass.

"You okay there, sweetie?" he asked me.

"Yeah, fine. Thank you."

He grunted. "Don't mention it."

He waved for another drink and Esme came over. She'd been so busy she'd missed the whole thing, for which I was glad.

"You can put that on my tab," I said to her as she poured him another and I handed over my card.

He tried to protest, but I wouldn't let him.

"We need more men like you in the world." That made him laugh so hard he had a coughing fit and couldn't stop wheezing.

"That's definitely not true, but thank you anyway, sweetheart."

It was time to go. I couldn't stand to be in Wyatt's presence anymore.

I waved down Esme again.

"Hey, I'm going to head out. I'll be up for a while, so message me when you get a chance."

She gave me a wink.

"Will do."

"Oh, and thanks for the drink. I'd definitely like to have that one again."

"You got it."

I didn't look at Wyatt's group as I left. I didn't want to give him the satisfaction. I'd rather die than let him know he'd rattled me. Fucker.

Knowing that I had something to hold over his head wasn't as satisfying as I'd thought. All I could think about as I drove back home was how satisfying it would have been to smash his face into the bar. He deserved it for so many reasons.

.

Chapter Eleven

"So, how are things going?" Mom asked at dinner the next night. She said she was tired, so I'd ordered lasagna and Greek salad that she loved from the restaurant twenty minutes outside Castleton.

"Oh, they're going," I said, just before I shoved a giant bite of lasagna in my mouth and promptly choked on it. Mom stared at me as I tried to get my breath back and wipe my watering eyes.

"You really need to take smaller bites," she said.

"I'll keep that in mind."

"So," she said, dabbing at her mouth with her napkin, "how are things going?"

My fork paused in midair. I knew that tone. She knew something. How much, I was going to have to find out.

The two of us locked eyes as we waited for the other one to break.

My mom had many years more of practice, so I ended up caving.

"Okay, what do you know?" I asked.

She sat back in her chair, her smile full of smugness. I

stabbed at my lasagna with my fork, wishing this conversation wasn't going to make me lose my appetite.

"Well, I got not one, but three messages informing me that my daughter was looking extremely cozy with the local bartender at the beach. Would you care to elaborate and fill in the blanks?"

Phew. Okay. So far she just knew that I'd gone to the beach with Esme. As long as she didn't know that Esme had stayed over. That part I'd rather keep between me and Esme.

"Yes, we went to the beach together. We hung out. I don't know." I could feel myself melting under her scrutiny.

"Do you think it's something serious?" she asked.

"I don't know, it wasn't even a date. We just hung out. No definitions. I don't know." I needed to stop saying that or she was going to get suspicious.

"She's a nice girl. I always thought it was so wonderful how she stayed with her father and took care of him." She gave me a pointed look, as if I hadn't done the exact same thing.

My mom was never going to forgive me for moving out, even though I was a full-ass adult who needed her own space. Lots of parents would be thrilled to have independent children, but not mine.

"Yeah, they're really close," I said, treading lightly. If I wasn't careful, this conversation was going to turn into a guilt trip, and I didn't need that.

"Well, if you do decide that you're going to date her, I approve." As if I needed her permission. Plus, she'd approved of Wyatt and look how that had turned out. Mom was not the best judge of character at all.

"Thanks," I said. "I have no idea if it will go anywhere, but I really like her." I shouldn't have admitted that, but it was too late to take it back.

"I'm still holding out hope for Wyatt, but Esme is a good girl."

I bit back a scream and covered by noisily getting up from the table and taking my dishes to the sink.

"I'm really tired, so I'm going to head out," I said, pulling out a container so I could take some of the lasagna home.

"Okay," Mom said, coming up behind me and giving me a hug. "It's good to see you. And thanks for bringing me dinner."

I turned around and hugged her back.

"You're welcome, Mom. Always."

Even though she was hard to love, at the end of the day, I did love her.

~

I NEED a drink I sent to Esme as soon as I got home with my leftover lasagna.

I get off at one. Can you wait?

There was absolutely no way I was going to be able to stay awake until one in the morning.

Absolutely I said.

~

MY PLAN TO take a nap before Esme came over was smart in theory, but in practice I passed out on the couch and woke up to someone knocking on my door.

For a second I was terrified, and then I woke up enough to remember that I'd invited Esme to come over and bring drinks.

"Come in," I said, my voice thick with sleep. I'd left my door unlocked on purpose.

"Hey," Esme said in a soft voice, poking her head in. "Did I wake you up?"

"No," I lied, sitting up on the couch and combing my hair with my fingers before checking to make sure I didn't have any crusties in the corners of my eyes.

"Hey, Potato," Esme said, giving the cat some attention before coming over to the couch and sitting down.

"I'm sorry, I should have sent a message to make sure you were awake," she said, putting my feet in her lap.

"No, it's fine."

The night was warm and she had glitter on her eyelids that was a little smudged after a long shift.

Looking at her made something deep in my chest ache in the most wonderful way.

"I brought you a little something. Let me go mix it up and I'll be right back."

Potato followed her to supervise while I tried to get myself a little more perky.

"I figured since I kept you up, the least I can do is make up for it," she said as she came back with two mugs, which I didn't expect.

"Here we go. Frozen spiked cocoa." She handed me one of the cold mugs and I sipped through the straw. The chocolate hit me first, along with the coldness. I was a little sweaty from my nap, so it was a nice change. Then a little hint of booze hit me as I swallowed.

"This is perfect," I said, trying not to suck down the whole thing at once.

"I'm sorry I woke you," she said, holding her drink in one hand, and rubbing my foot absentmindedly with the other.

"It's okay. It's worth it. How was work?"

We lightly chatted as I finished my drink. The alcohol went to my head and I started to feel sleepy and warm again.

"Do you want to stay over?" I asked through a yawn. I was absolutely done and if I didn't go to bed now, I was going to be too tired to walk there.

"No, I should get home. But maybe this weekend? As long as you're okay if I come a little late. Not this late. I've changed my hours a little, so I'll be getting off at seven instead on Thursday nights."

That was unexpected.

"They're also going to hire an extra bartender for the summer, so I'll be able to cut back a little bit more. Maybe even take off two whole days a week. I literally don't remember the last time I had two days off in a row."

My heart leapt at the idea of her working less, because it meant she might have more time to spend with me. It was probably selfish to want to claim those hours already, but I couldn't help it.

"That would be great," I said, my words slurring together from tiredness and the boozy cocoa.

"Okay, time to get you to bed. Come on." I protested, but she leaned down and got me up, having me lean on her as she walked us both to my bedroom.

Esme pulled some pajamas out of my drawer and set them down next to me.

"I know I should leave you to sleep, but I really don't want to," she said.

My eyes fluttered open and closed as I tried everything to stay awake to keep looking at her.

"Okay," I said. Or at least that was what I meant to say.

Esme sighed and stood up, coming over to give me a kiss on the forehead.

"Get some sleep, Paige. We'll talk tomorrow."

I fell asleep before I could answer her.

"SHE'S COMING over tonight and bringing me dinner. We're going to do a movie night," I said to Em when she came to visit me during her lunch break to get the details on further developments with Esme.

"I'm so jealous. I'm sorry, but I believe in honesty." She rested her chin in her hand and pouted.

"Sorry, she doesn't have any sisters I could set you up with. Let me find out about cousins or other relatives?"

"It's the least you can do," Em said.

"You got it."

"So, what are you going to watch? You know how much I judge people on their taste in movies." This was true. She'd said she wasn't sure if she could be friends with me after I mentioned one of my terrible favorites. We'd already had a solid friendship at the time, so I wasn't totally in danger of losing her, but she was as bad about movies as some people were about zodiac signs.

"All of the movies in the 'historical drama with lesbian yearning' collection. With a romcom at the end to lighten things up," I said.

Esme and I had spent a considerable amount of time and effort to craft the perfect movie night. Since I was supplying the house, she was bringing dinner. Staying over hadn't been discussed because I was too much of a baby to ask her to. I didn't want to beg, and I didn't want to make her feel like she had to. A conundrum, for sure. Guess I'd just see what the vibe was tonight and we could decide then.

"Sounds lovely," Em said with a wistful sigh, before finishing her sandwich and realizing she had to go back to work.

"Oh, I'll leave you with this little tidbit: Gretchen clogged the toilet at my parent's house and we had to call a plumber."

I gagged and made a face at her.

"I really didn't need to know any of that, thank you."

Em gave me a little smile and wave as she headed back to the office. I shivered and tried to get the idea of Gretchen and clogged toilets out of my brain.

~

"SO, I could tell you that I made this, but that would be a lie. I stopped at the store and bought everything pre-made," Esme said when she showed up at my place later that night.

"Dad has really gotten into making these food kits, so we're having fajitas and a black bean and corn salad, and tres leches for dessert with some fresh strawberries." All of that sounded absolutely amazing, so I stepped aside and let Esme get everything heated up and ready as she talked about her day and filled me in on local gossip.

"You know Kim Carpenter, right?"

I nodded as I leaned on the counter and she stirred the chicken and peppers in a pan to get warm. The tortillas were doing their thing in the oven. I kept sneaking little bites from the bean and corn salad.

"Well, she finally threw her deadbeat husband out and she's literally living her best life. She's like a completely different person. Remember how her face was always so gray and she never smiled? She came into the bar and I swear, I didn't recognize her. Dropping that loser has done wonders for her skin."

She pulled out the tortillas and then arranged everything for me on a plate.

"And what's her deadbeat husband doing?" I asked.

"If gossip is to be believed, her sister, Erica."

"Oh, gross," I said as we sat down on the couch. Esme had also brought margarita mix and had made us up some virgin drinks.

"Are you ready for intense eye contact?" I asked as I queued up the first movie.

"Bring it," she said.

~

"I LOVE how you can watch a movie and they have sex and it's like, meh, but then you watch something like this and you lose your mind every time their hands touch," Esme said, after we finished the first movie and broke out the cake.

"That's the power of the period drama. If you had eye contact back then, it was basically like fucking."

Esme gazed at me and didn't look away. My face heated and I wasn't thinking about cake anymore.

Esme slowly smiled. "How was it for you?"

I pretended to fan myself. "If I smoked, I'd need a cigarette right about now."

"I've got an old vape pen in my car if you want."

I shook my head. "No, I'm good. Do you vape?"

"Used to. And I smoked. I know, I know, but everyone at the restaurant did, so I guess I caved to peer pressure. How sad is that?"

"Not sad at all. Have I told you about my mom and her pyramid schemes?"

Esme burst out laughing and almost dropped her cake plate.

"No, tell me."

It hadn't been in my seduction plan to tell Esme about my mother and her penchant for getting scammed, but once she expressed an interest, I opened my mouth and couldn't shut up. Sure, I'd told Linley and Em about it, but I didn't go into all the details and my frustration with everything.

"My dad used to buy too much stuff from TV infomercials. We'd get these boxes that would just show up and I'd have no idea what the hell was going to be in them. It was everything from knives to clothing to purses, for some reason? I mean, I think he was buying the stuff for me, but it wasn't anything I wanted? Bless him. He tried. Plus, now we have some really great cookware, so I shouldn't complain."

"Your dad and my mom should be friends," I said.

"Maybe we can make that happen. I have been trying to get him out more. She wouldn't try to recruit him into a scam, would she?"

I nodded. "Oh, she absolutely would."

"Never mind," Esme said with a laugh.

We moved on to the next movie and just a few minutes in, Esme put her arm around me and I leaned into her. Too bad it was so warm that we couldn't share a blanket.

Her fingers drifted from my shoulder to the ends of my hair.

I tried to focus on the film, but having Esme so close was distracting. I also couldn't stop imagining us sitting together like this beyond tonight. She'd brought an extra bag with her, but it was just the regular bag she carried all the time, so I didn't think it had any overnight items in it. I still hoped that it did.

"Do you mind if I stay tonight? It's absolutely fine if the answer is no. I brought my stuff, just in case," she said, as if she'd read my mind.

"Yes, you can stay." I had to stop myself from adding "forever" onto the end of that sentence. It was way too early for any kind of sentiment like that.

"If I had to be married to these annoying men, I think I'd make out with a lady too," Esme said, and I settled further into her. "Oh, and I brought my special haircare so I don't have to be threatened with the garbage you have in your shower right now."

I sat up, pretending to be offended.

"You are awfully judgmental about my hair products."

Esme ran her hands through her hair. "This takes a lot of maintenance. It's a sacrifice I'm willing to make."

It was true that she did have incredible hair. I let my hand slide through her silky hair, all the way to the ends.

"You make me want to grow out my hair again, but I hate

it when my hair is long," I said. I'd done the chop earlier this year, and I did not want to go back anytime soon.

"You can always get wigs. I've got a few."

"Really?" I said, completely distracted from the movie by the image of Esme in a wig. "Can I get some more details about these wigs?"

Esme gave me a secretive smile.

"Next time I'll bring one and show you."

I almost slid off the couch and onto the floor.

What was she doing to me?

"I'm learning all kinds of things about you, Esme."

"And you're bound to learn many more," she said, as I snuggled into her again and tried to go back to watching the movie.

The women in the movie were nothing to the woman sitting beside me. I kept glancing at her from the corner of my eye, but she seemed to be engrossed with what was playing on the TV.

I wanted her. I wanted her in an aching, painful way. Every place she touched me was on fire.

"Oh, there they go," she said, and I realized she was talking about the movie. The characters had finally succumbed to their lust and started tearing each other's corsets off.

In any other circumstances, I would be paying attention to the sexy content, but it just made me wish I was taking a corset off Esme. Something told me she had one in her closet.

"Makes you think," I said, and she looked at me.

"Think about what?"

"Think that we could be doing the same thing right now," I said, touching her face.

Esme looked at the screen and back to me.

"You're right. Reality is better than fiction sometimes." Without another word, she took the remote, turned off the movie, and stood up, almost dumping me on the floor in the process.

"Fuck yeah," I said, scrambling to get my feet under me as she backed toward my bedroom, her smile dark and inviting.

I almost tripped, but I made it to her and then it was a race to see who could get their clothes off the fastest while trading breathless kisses.

Esme lay back on the bed and then threw a few of my pillows on the floor.

"My sunburn doesn't hurt anymore," she said as I devoured her with my eyes.

"That's good," I said, "because I have so many plans for you."

She tilted her chin up, as if it was a challenge. "Show me."

I DID SHOW HER. I reached into my bag of tricks and pulled anything out I thought she might like.

"You're really good at that," she said, as I withdrew my fingers from inside her after her fourth orgasm.

"Thank you," I said, pretending to take a bow.

"I've been blessed with talented fingers and a talented tongue." I stuck said tongue out at her and did a few little maneuvers with it.

"Rude. Extremely rude," she said.

Esme had her own sexy secrets, and it turned out that our adventurous sides were evenly matched. Her eyes lit up when I brought out my toy box.

"You would not believe what I have to do to hide mine from my dad. He sometimes cleans in my room, so I've had to take extreme measures," she said when we were taking a break and decided to take a shower.

"I usually take the batteries out of my vibrators, but once, I forgot one. Of course it somehow turned itself on while my mom was having a party at our house. I blame mean ghosts trying to fuck with me. It was in a drawer, and it was so loud."

Esme was trying not to laugh, but completely failing. I didn't blame her, it was a hilarious story. I'd be laughing if it hadn't happened to me.

"There was a lull in the conversation and someone said 'what's that?' and I basically sprinted to my room to turn it off before my mom could get there ahead of me. I shut the door right in her face and she got mad, but at least we never had to speak of it again. She pretends that it never happened and so do I."

I turned the shower on and Esme brought out her hair stuff.

"I'm trusting you with this," I said. "Meaning my hair." It might not be as pretty or as long as hers, but I did value it.

"You'll be fine, I swear. It's all-natural stuff. See?" She showed me the container and then shoved me under the spray to wet down my hair before slathering the stuff on and then turning so I could do the same for her.

We both rinsed the stuff out after a few minutes and then she wrapped herself in one of my towels and I put on a robe.

"I meant to bring a robe, but I completely forgot. Next time," she said. I had to fight to not scream with excitement. This meant that she wanted to come over again. This was starting to be something.

She let me help her squeeze the water out of her hair and then braid it back for her.

"Wow, I am bad at braiding on another person. I'm so used to doing it on myself, but this is different." I combed out the braid I'd started and attempted it again.

"It doesn't have to be perfect," she said, looking over her shoulder at me.

"I know. But I want it to look good."

I wanted it to look good for her. I couldn't articulate to her why this mattered to me.

Potato chose that moment to wander in and see what the hell we were doing. For a curious animal, he generally stayed away from my bedroom when he heard the buzz of a vibrator.

Good kitty.

"Hey, sweet boy," Esme said, as Potato jumped on the bed for attention.

"Sometimes I think I should get him a friend so he's not lonely," I said. "I feel so bad that I'm gone for work all the time. I want a dog, but I don't have the time for one."

"I could bring Stormy over," Esme said. "I feel bad leaving her alone too. She goes to doggie daycare during the day, and then Dad picks her up most days. Do you think Potato would be okay with having her come over?"

Potato looked at me as if he knew we were talking about him.

"Potato has met dogs before. I think he'd be fine, but we won't know for sure until we try," I said.

I really hoped Potato wouldn't attack her dog. That might make our relationship complicated.

"I do have one question about dogs," Esme said.

"What's that?" I asked.

"Would you let Stormy sleep in this bed?"

"I mean, Potato does whatever the hell he wants, so I don't see how that's any different."

Esme rubbed Potato's belly. "That's because you don't have to share a bed with a large dog on a regular basis. When I got her, I literally bought a bigger bed so I wouldn't have to sleep on the floor."

I had definitely spent my fair share of nights sleeping badly because of Potato. For a while, he decided that he needed to sleep on my head like a hat. That had been rough.

"Stormy is welcome here," I said, patting the bed.

"And me?" Esme asked. "Am I welcome in your bed?"

"Obviously," I said, rolling my eyes. "You're literally in it right now."

"I like your bed and I like being in it. I foresee spending a lot of time here." She lay back, putting her hands behind her head.

"Even with all my pillows?"

"Even with the pillows," she said, and then hit me with one of them.

Potato ran for the safety of the bathroom as I attempted to defend myself against the pillow onslaught.

In the end, Esme had better pillow fight technique and I ended up just curling up into a ball on the bed and begging for mercy.

"Please no more," I said, my voice muffled.

"Okay," she said with a sigh. "I guess I'll just go, then."

I looked up as she started to get out of bed, and I lunged to grab her arm.

"No, don't go. Come baacckkkkkkk." She looked down at me and smiled before giving me a kiss.

"Okay, I'll stay."

"You're easy to convince," I said.

Chapter Twelve

"I HAVE TO SHOW YOU SOMETHING," Linley said on Saturday when I went to her place to hang out. I loved my cottage, but her place was nice. Like, *nice* nice. Shiny and new and granite and stainless. She'd done what she could to make the space cozy with tons and tons of framed pictures and art and cute lamps.

"As long as it's not, like, a bleeding wound, go ahead and show me," I said, sipping from the late she'd made me from a fancy coffee machine her parents had gotten her for Christmas last year.

"It's not a wound," she said, and then presented me with…

"Oh my god, it is a pangolin."

In my hands was the tiniest, most perfect little pangolin, standing on its legs and holding its paws? Feet? together. It even had a little worried look in its eyes.

"I may have mentioned them on our date and then he showed up with this in a box."

I set the little creature down on the counter and shook my head.

"Unbelievable. He should make more and sell them online," I said.

"I think he might." Her smile was soft and dreamy and I could tell she was really in deep with this guy.

"When do I get to meet him? I know your mom is all over that, but I'd like to see the two of you together. Give my approval," I said.

Linley sipped her coffee and looked at me over the rim of her cup. "Speaking of that, he's actually coming over tomorrow for the first time. I talked Mom into letting me have Monday off, so he's going to stay the night."

"Ohhhhh, the first sleepover. When you find out if he snores or talks in his sleep. A pivotal moment in any relationship," I said.

She looked down at the little carved pangolin. "Does Esme snore?"

I'd spent two nights with her at this point, and most of those nights had been taken up with sex and very little sleep.

"I don't remember," I said.

"If she did, you'd remember."

That was a good point.

"The other question is, do *you* snore?" she said.

"No," I said defensively. Then I thought about it for a moment. "Well, no one has ever said anything. If I did snore, I'm pretty sure Wyatt would have bitched about it. Did I ever tell you he used to narrate his dreams?"

It had scared the shit out of me the first night I'd stayed with him and I'd awoken when he'd started talking. That dream was a Lord of the Rings style quest sort of thing. Turned out to be a reoccurring dream of his and I actually considered writing some of it down and maybe making a book out of it. I might still do that.

I helped Linley plan her strategy, including wardrobe (down to her underwear) for the upcoming date.

"I know I want to have him to myself for just a little while longer and get through this first overnight, but after this weekend, I will definitely ask him if he wants to make a plan to have a group thing with you and Em. I'm still holding my mom off, so don't say anything in case she might find out."

She looked around nervously, as if her mother was going to pop out from one of the cabinets. I wouldn't put it past her.

"I won't say a word," I said, pretending to zip my lips and throw away the key.

"I'm serious. She can never find out that Gray met my friends before he met her. My dad doesn't care, but my mom sure does." Linley gripped my arm so had I was afraid she was going to leave marks.

"It's fine. She's not going to find out. And even if she does, just say something about marriage or rings and she'll get distracted." Finally, Linley let go of me and nodded.

"Yeah, that's a good plan. It's a good plan for anything, really." That was true. Maybe I'd use that one on my mom.

"So, things are good with Esme?" she asked.

"Good. *Really* good." My face hurt from smiling, honestly. In random moments, I'd just think about something Esme had said, or the way she smiled, or I'd see something that would make her laugh and I'd completely forget about what I was supposed to be doing. I'd already started keeping even better spreadsheets of my deadlines so I didn't fuck too much up. It was all well and good to get distracted when I was doing the dishes, but it was another thing to mess up and piss off a client that was paying me a lot of money to do a job.

Linley warmed a cinnamon roll in the microwave for me as I blathered on and on about Esme. I knew I was probably telling her too much, and being too excessive, but I couldn't stop myself.

"You sound happy," Linley said, when I took a pause to eat.

"Do I?" I asked, my mouth full.

"Yeah, you do. I know I was a little negative when you first told me about this plan, but it looks like everything worked out in the end anyway."

"Yeah," I said, swallowing, but unable to swallow the lump of discomfort that I had whenever I thought about how things with Esme began with a lie. A plan. A silly plan, in hindsight, but still. I'd wanted to use her to one-up Wyatt. I felt gross whenever I thought about it, so I tried not to think about it. That worked most of the time, but every now and then, I'd remember and feel awful.

No matter what happened with Esme, she could never find out about it. I couldn't let her know I was the kind of person who would make a plan like that. It would change everything about how she saw me.

"Don't worry. You figured out it was a mistake. We all make mistakes, Paige." Linley gave me a hug and then another cinnamon roll.

"OKAY, I'm going to hold her and then you can bring Potato in," Esme said the following Tuesday when she brought Stormy over to meet Potato. We also had another date night planned. In two weeks, she was cutting back her hours, so we'd be able to have more dates and she'd have more time to devote to book collecting and her blog. Summer was in full swing and all I saw were beach days and lobster dinners and sweaty nights and lazy afternoons out in front of us.

"Okay," I said, going to get Potato as Esme brought in Stormy. She was so pretty and friendly, and I really hoped Potato wasn't going to freak out about a husky in his house.

I led Potato into the room where Esme was holding Stormy. Stormy perked up at the sight of me and then Potato. As soon as he saw the dog, Potato stopped in his tracks, and twitched his tail. He didn't seem stressed, just curious.

Stormy wagged her tail and seemed to want to come over to see about the new friend.

"That's Stormy," I said to Potato. "She's a new friend."

Potato looked up at me and then skipped over to Stormy to investigate. Stormy sniffed, but didn't attack Potato. Both Esme and I watched our respective pets take their measure of each other. There was lots of sniffing and testing and then Stormy lay on the floor and Potato started licking her ears.

"I think that's a good sign?" I said. Stormy jumped up and got in a playful stance and then started moving from side to side. Potato did the same and then they were chasing each other through the house.

"Okay then," Esme said with a laugh. "They're going to sleep good tonight."

Stormy and Potato chased each other for a little while and then curled up on Potato's bed and fell asleep together, Stormy curled protectively around Potato.

"I can never get enough pictures of this cuteness," Esme said as we both took a million shots.

"I was convinced they were going to hate each other," I said. "Potato is very particular."

"So is Stormy. She's a complete diva most of the time, but maybe that's why they're matched for each other." She looked at me and I couldn't help but lean over and kiss her.

"I don't know what I would have done if they hadn't gotten along. That would have been awful," I said. It had been a serious concern when I realized that Esme and I were getting closer and closer. That definitely would have been a bad omen.

"Now that we've got that all sorted out," Esme said, breaking the kiss and pushing me toward the couch, "we can get onto the second thing I came over for."

"Is it these?" I asked, yanking my shirt up. I wasn't wearing a bra, mostly because it was hot and I figured I was going to take it off anyway. It paid to be efficient.

Esme smiled. "They're definitely part of my plans."

At the mention of "plans," I froze. I didn't know why that word made me think of how we'd started, but it did and then I was immediately taken out of the moment. I tried to cover, but Esme noticed immediately.

"What's wrong? Are you okay?" I covered my boobs back up and shook my head.

"No, I'm fine. I just forgot about a work deadline and I need to send an email." I had pulled this answer completely out of my ass, but it was plausible.

"Okay," Esme said, moving back from me. "Do you need me to go?"

I grabbed her arm. "NO!" Ugh, tone down the desperation, Paige. "No, just give me a minute and I'll be back." I needed that time to get myself together anyway.

Esme went to pet Stormy as I pulled out my computer and pretended to type out an email and get my heart to stop pounding.

Once I had myself back under control, I shut my computer.

"So," I said, walking over to her. "Where were we?" A tiny voice of guilt whispered in my ear, but I ignored it as Esme pushed me toward the couch again and we started right where we left off.

"I REALLY LIKE YOU, PAIGE," Esme said later, as we lay in bed with Potato and Stormy. She'd been right to worry about the bed being big enough for all of us. I'd had to sacrifice more pillows to give the dog enough space to stretch out.

Esme's legs were entwined with mine and my nose was mere millimeters from hers.

"I really like you, Esme. A lot. In case that wasn't clear." My heart felt like it was going to crack my ribs.

"No, it's pretty clear. I just wanted to make sure that you knew I'm really happy with you. And if you wanted to talk about what this means, I'm open to that. If you're not, then I'm happy to keep hanging out with you like this."

She was so good. So damn good.

"I'm ready to have that conversation," I blurted out. Other people might have said this was fast, but when it came to relationships, it was pretty much my only speed.

"Perfect," she said, snuggling even closer. "Are you thinking you want to make things official?"

"Definitely," I said. "I'd love to be official with you, Esme."

She kissed me. "That's what I want too."

Kissing led to other things, and the animals were extremely upset when we kicked them out again, but we let them come back after we took a quick shower.

"You can store stuff here, if you need to," I said. "I can clear you a spot in my dresser."

Esme raised one eyebrow. "I'm getting a drawer already?"

"Of course, you're worth it."

She kissed my nose. "You're so sweet. Why hadn't I ever seen it before?"

It was strange, that we'd grown up in this town always seeing each other, but never having our paths cross until now.

"You were worth the wait," I said.

"You too."

If only it hadn't been revenge on my shitty ex that had made me see her for who she was. If only I'd come to that realization on my own. She'd been right there the whole time.

As I lay there between Esme and a warm dog with barely enough space to stretch out my body, I wondered if I was doing the right thing. If I was a bad person. If I deserved her. If I should tell her the truth.

I played out all the scenarios in my head, again, as I had dozens of times. That was the part I hadn't planned initially. What would happen after I got my revenge. Who I would hurt in the process.

It was a struggle not to feel like a complete monster for even considering it.

I'd been so distracted by my rage toward Wyatt that I'd let it cloud my judgment. Fucking Wyatt. Ruined everything again. Why couldn't he just get hit by a bus or move to another planet?

Esme made a little humming noise in her sleep and moved closer to me. I held her close and tried to fall asleep.

THE NEXT MORNING was a mess of a dog, a cat, some burned bacon, and pancake batter everywhere.

"I'm sorry," I said, as Esme threw the burned bacon in the trash as I opened the windows and waved a dish towel to disperse the smoke from the oven.

"It's not your fault. I did kind of distract you." That was fair. It was hard to focus on cooking bacon when your girl-friend was finger-fucking you up against the fridge.

"Take two," I said, getting out another pan and covering it with tinfoil to put in the oven.

"You know, my dad has an air fryer and it makes the best bacon. I'll bring it over next time."

She put her arms around me and kissed the back of my neck. I completely forgot what I was doing as Esme did her best to distract me from breakfast again.

Eventually, we got everything together and Esme made us breakfast mocktails.

"I could definitely get used to this," I said, sipping my drink as we lounged on the couch and watched gay cartoons while our pets chased each other around the room.

"Me too," she said. "I really, really like being with you, Paige. And I'm definitely thinking that it's time I got my own place."

That was surprising. She'd been with her dad so long and they were so close, I'd thought she was at least somewhat happy there. Not like me and my mom who were better off living apart.

"Yeah?" I said.

"Yeah. I want to have you over and not worry about him walking in to ask if we need anything." She shuddered. "Let's just say he's caught me more times than I'd like to speak about."

"Yikes," I said. "Yeah, get your own place. I think there are units available in Linley's building. I can get her to put in a good word for you," I said. Esme waved me off.

"No worries, I know the owner. He comes into the bar all the time. In fact, he's been telling me that anytime I want to move in, just say the word. He's good people." Huh. Guess she did have friends in high places.

"Well, if you need any help moving in, I have a car and I'm good at lifting pillows." I flexed and she laughed.

"No, no, I'm definitely hiring movers. No need for you to do that, but I appreciate the offer so much." She kissed me and her lips tasted of warm butter and syrup. Delicious.

At Esme's suggestion, we took Stormy out for a walk, and I showed her all the cute little side roads and other cottages and cabins near mine. There was even a micro beach with rocky sand that wasn't great for lounging, but had pieces of driftwood for sitting, and she let Stormy off the leash to run into the water and chase sticks that we threw.

"It really is beautiful here," she said, staring up at the sky.

I couldn't stop staring at her. The sun hit the red highlights in her hair, and her skin glowed. Stunning. Sometimes I couldn't believe she was real.

Esme sighed and put her head on my shoulder. In that moment, all was right and good in the world.

I should have known it wasn't going to last.

Chapter Thirteen

Esme and I had lunch together, and then she said she needed to do some stuff for her dad and I definitely needed to catch up on work.

"Come to the bar tonight. Please?" As if she really had to ask.

"Of course I will," I said, kissing her goodbye.

I was in the midst of doing a video transcription when a message from Linley came through.

I need to tell you something, but I'm not sure if I should tell you.

What the hell did that mean? I called her for an explanation.

"What's going on? Are you okay? Are your parents okay?" My mind went immediately to death and destruction.

"Yes, I'm fine. Everyone's fine. Sorry. I shouldn't have written that message like that," she said.

Trembling, I held the phone tight to my ear.

"What's going on?" I asked.

"Are you sitting down?"

Fuck. What was it?

"Yes, I'm on the couch, you'd better fill in me right now, or else I'm going to come over there and make you tell me," I said.

"Okay, I'll say it. Gretchen is pregnant. That's probably against baker-customer privilege to tell you, but whatever. She came in to order a cake. She's going to surprise Wyatt. I'm so sorry, Paige. Are you okay?"

I burst out laughing. The sound was loud, even to me, and I couldn't seem to stop laughing.

"She's pregnant! Of course she is!" I wiped the tears streaming from my face and stood up.

"You've got to be fucking kidding me!" I screamed. Potato ran into the bedroom to get away from me.

I couldn't get my breathing or heartrate back to normal. I couldn't figure out what my body wanted to do.

"I'm so sorry. I shouldn't have told you on the phone. I should have done it in person, but I was freaking out and I didn't want you to hear it from anyone else. Do you need me to come over?" she asked.

I didn't know what I needed. Soon, the laughing turned to tears, and at some point Linley said she was coming over and to stay on the line with her. I curled into myself, clutching the phone to my ear like a life raft.

It didn't take Linley long to make it to my door and soon I was wrapped in a hug that smelled of yeast and fresh strawberries.

By that point my crying had subsided a little, and all I wanted to do was either go to sleep or scream forever.

"I'm so sorry, Paige." Linley rubbed my back and held me for as long as I needed it.

A body can only cry for so long, but it felt like forever before I could pull back from Linley and take a full breath again.

She was there with tissues and support.

"I don't even know why I'm so upset?" I said. "It's not like I wanted to have a baby with him. Well, at least not right now."

If I said I hadn't thought about it, I would be lying. Of course I'd planned out my future with Wyatt. He'd take over the insurance company and I'd keep doing my thing and we'd have a lovely house just outside of town with two or three kids and a golden retriever. Wyatt would have a boat and take the kids fishing on the weekends. I'd have a garden and grow tomatoes and volunteer at the library.

When he'd ended things, all of those visions disappeared. Evaporated. The house, the kids, the dog, the life, gone.

Now someone else was going to have that life. Have his baby.

"I can't believe this is happening," I said.

"I know. I just can't picture Gretchen as a mom. She's going to have to think about someone other than herself, for once. And she'll have to give up drinking on the weekends," she said.

I guess that was something.

"That poor baby," I said. Kid was doomed, with parents like that.

"Seriously. Can you imagine those being your parents? I can't imagine what awful name Gretchen is already picking out," Linley said.

I blew my nose and suddenly lost all of my energy.

"I feel like I need a nap now," I said.

"Take a warm bath with lots of candles and Epsom salts," Linley said. "And I'll bring you dinner."

I was so lucky to have her as a friend.

"Wait, does Em know?" I asked. She was going to lose it when she found out she was going to be an aunt.

Linley shook her head. "No, no one knows, other than me. And I wouldn't have even known if I hadn't looked at the name and address on the order. Honestly, it seems a little tacky."

It kind of was.

"How far along is she?" I asked. Did I even want to know?

"Not sure. The order came through online. I'm supposed to drop it off at Gretchen's before five, so I'm guessing she's going to have a party or something," she said.

That sounded about right. I wanted to message Em and ask her if she'd been invited to a party with her parents and Wyatt and Gretchen, but then she'd get suspicious.

"Fuck, this is all bizarre. I don't think it's really sunk in yet," I said.

It probably wouldn't until I saw Gretchen with a visible belly. That was next to impossible to picture.

"You go take your bath, I'll bring you food, and then you can come over tonight, if you want," she said.

"Thank you. I promised I'd see Esme at the bar, so I'll stop by there for a drink before I head over."

We had a plan, and that was something. Linley gave me another hug before she left.

Taking her advice, I got myself into the tub with soothing music and candles and I also added a tray of snacks because I wanted to be fancy.

It didn't fix all my problems, but it did make me feel a tiny bit better. The tiniest bit.

Linley dropped off dinner, and I didn't ask her if she was on her way to drop of Gretchen's cake. I also didn't ask what she'd frosted on it to announce the pregnancy. Probably something really cliché and basic. Gretchen didn't have a whole lot of imagination. I'd had art class with her one semester, I should know.

Deciding that one bath wasn't enough, I actually got back in the tub and had dinner there. I emerged a full-body prune, but I didn't care. I dried my hair and pinned it back before putting on a loose dress and heading out to the bar to see Esme.

"Hey," I said, leaning over the bar and giving her a smile that felt forced.

"Hey," she said, beaming and then her face fell after looking at me for more than a moment.

"What's wrong?" she asked immediately.

I'd done my best to take down the puffiness of my eyes after crying so much, but I guess I hadn't done a good enough job.

"It's nothing," I said.

She reached across the bar and took my hands.

"No, tell me. We can go in the back where it's quiet."

I shook my head. "It's fine. I'm fine. Just got some interesting news."

Her eyes went wide. "Is your mom okay?"

I squeezed her hands. "Yes, yes. It's really not a big deal. Just something that had me a little upset, but I'm here with you now to cheer me up."

I attempted another smile, and it felt a little bit better.

"Are you sure?" she asked.

I nodded.

"Okay then. How about a drink?" She smiled softly.

"Yes, please." I sat on a stool and watched as Esme made me a drink. I was distracted from watching my bartender work by a loud shrieking noise and cheering coming from the restaurant section. Must be someone's birthday. I glanced over and had to grip the bar so I didn't fall off my stool as I watched Wyatt's parents and Gretchen's parents hug the parents-to-be. I guess Em hadn't been invited to the announcement.

Well, there was the cake. It was too far away for me to read, but I was sure Linley had done a beautiful job.

Gretchen had her arms around Wyatt and a huge smile on her face. He was grinning as well, but I knew him well enough to know that he was flipping out inside. He kept clenching and unclenching one fist at his side. His parents looked stunned, but happy.

Something inside me broke and I needed to get away from this place. I somehow got my feet under me and stumbled toward the back door of the bar that led to the little smoking area that had some rickety picnic tables, a few rotted lawn chairs, and a sad string of party lights.

I put my hands on my knees and tried to stop myself from hyperventilating. A warm hand rested on my back, but I was too worked up to worry about it.

"Hey, what's wrong, Paige? I saw you run out and I'm really getting worried about you."

Esme's voice was tight with concern as her hand worked in soothing circles.

I wasn't in danger of hyperventilating or passing out anymore, and I didn't think there were enough tears left in my body, so I just kind of fell into the nearest chair.

Esme crouched next to me and moved my hair out of my face.

"What happened?" she asked.

There was no way to pass my reaction off anymore as "nothing."

"I don't know if you saw in there, but my ex, Wyatt apparently knocked up Gretchen and they brought both their parents here to celebrate. I found out earlier because Linley made the cake and told me. I'm sorry I didn't tell you. I don't know why I didn't," I said.

I should have told her, but I hadn't wanted to distract her from work, or act like I was making a bigger deal out this than it was.

"I'm sorry, Paige. That must be awful to see them right in your face like that," she said.

Her hand continued to stroke my shoulder.

"It's not like I'm still in love with him or want him back. He can choke, for all I care, but it was still a lot to see that. It just hurts. I thought I was really over him." With the exception of the whole revenge plot that she didn't know about.

"Having this reaction doesn't mean anything other than you're hurting, and that's okay. It's normal to be upset about an ex," she said.

I guess that was true. It wasn't like I could just turn off the love switch when I wanted to. If I never saw Wyatt again, I would still have the memories of the time we'd spent together. The nights we'd shared. The good times we'd had.

"You're so good at this, Esme. I don't know how you do it, but every time I feel like shit, you manage to make me feel better," I said.

She just fluttered her hand.

"It's a gift."

I sat back in the chair and sighed. "I only came here to see you and have a drink, and then I was going over to Linley's for wallowing."

Esme stood up. "I think that's a great plan. Since you can't wallow with me, I'm glad you'll have someone to support your wallowing efforts. How about this? I'll bring your drink out here and then you can go around to your car without going inside again."

That sounded way better than my other plan, which was to go in and dump the cake on Wyatt's head. I'd probably get in trouble for that anyway.

"It's a plan," I said, and Esme came back a few moments later with a drink for me and a water for herself and we sat there as I finished my drink and she chattered about anything but Wyatt, Gretchen, or babies.

A few bar patrons came outside to smoke and talk as I finished my drink and tried not to think about what Wyatt was doing.

Would he and Gretchen get married? They didn't need to, obviously, but I wondered. They hadn't been seeing each other that long, and I didn't know what Gretchen's views on marriage were, but I could sure see her being one of those girls who spent their entire life planning for that one day. She would definitely be a bridezilla, for sure.

I finished my drink and Esme got called back to the bar, so she gave me a quick kiss. Batman happened to be having a smoke at the time and I could tell he saw, but he didn't make any comment. To be fair, Batman didn't comment on much of anything.

I snuck around to the front of the building and got into my car without once glancing back to see if Wyatt and Gretchen and their families we're still in there. It didn't matter.

Linley welcomed me with open arms and a huge cheesecake.

"Bless you, my friend," I said. "You will never guess who I saw tonight."

I flopped down on her couch and she set the cheesecake in front of me with a fork.

"Oh no," she said, connecting the dots immediately.

"Yup. I didn't get a close up of the cake, but I'm guessing they enjoyed it," I said, stabbing my fork in a corner of the cheesecake with fresh strawberries on top.

"I'm so sorry. You have the worst luck."

I filled her in on how I'd had to tell Esme about everything and how comforting she'd been.

"She really is a good one," Linley said, also dipping into the cheesecake with much smaller bites than mine. For me, this was medicinal cheesecake.

"Do you think she's going to have like, forty baby showers?" Linley asked.

"As many chances as she can get to be the center of attention? Absolutely," I said. Linley had also made tea, so I gulped down a cup of lavender tea, hoping that would calm me down. I had no idea how I was going to sleep tonight.

"Let's not talk about it anymore. There's nothing you can do."

That was true. No matter how much time I spent wallowing or crying or cursing at Wyatt, it wasn't going to change what had happened between us, or what was happening with him and Gretchen.

Even though it was hot, Linley put a blanket around my shoulders and put on a soothing baking show.

"I thought you hated this?" As a baker herself, she'd get all kinds of worked up when people were about to make a massive baking mistake.

"I know, but you like it," she said. "I'm just going to try and keep my commentary to myself."

I lifted the blanket so she could share it with me.

"No, yell all you want. It enhances the experience."

IN SPITE OF EVERYTHING, I ended up passing out on Linley's couch. The next thing I knew, I was waking up in her apartment and it was morning.

I got up and looked around, completely disoriented. Linley was gone, but there was a note on the coffee table that said she'd wanted to let me sleep, and that I could help myself to anything.

Poor Potato was probably starving, so as soon as I was awake enough, I got in my car and headed home.

I was greeted by a hungry and enraged furball.

"I know, I know, I'm sorry," I said, giving him pets and then rushing to fill his bowls.

Once fed, Potato let me know how much he'd missed me, so I guess I was forgiven.

I also had a few missed messages, including a few from Em.

Can you believe Gretchen is fucking pregnant?!

I replied that I couldn't, and that led to a flurry of messages back and forth while she gave me the full story.

As far as she knew, it was unintentional, but they were keeping it and Gretchen was moving in with him. No talk of marriage yet, but she didn't think it was out of the picture.

Can I come over tonight? I need to process this shit with someone.

I told her she could as long as I didn't have to cook. My night on Linley's couch hadn't been as restful as I needed, so I decided to take a short nap before starting my Monday.

That short nap turned into a much longer nap, and I was all messed up when I woke up later. After a fast breakfast and two cups of coffee, I headed to the café to get my work in.

Esme checked in to see how I was doing, and I said that I was better. She asked if she could come over after work, and I agreed. She had Tuesday completely off, but I had work, so she was going to bring Stormy and then just chill at my place while I did the work that I couldn't put off.

My life before Esme had been full, so fitting her in required work moving things around. It would mean taking fewer work projects, spending fewer hours on my computer. In the end, it was worth it. I was willing to make those cuts because she made me happy. My life had improved with her in it. Why wouldn't I want to have more time with her?

She was also re-prioritizing her life, and not just for me. We'd both gotten ourselves into ruts and hadn't realized it until we'd started spending time with each other.

My Monday was as productive as it was going to get after my weird morning, and with thinking about Wyatt and Gretchen.

Their news hit social media with pictures of them from the

night before at the restaurant. I tried not to look, but it was hard not to.

The cake was lovely, Linley had done an incredible job.

All the comments were congratulatory and excited and made me want to throw up. After a while, I closed the windows and forced myself to go back to work.

A very small, small part of me wished that I had somehow been able to get my revenge on Wyatt. Not with Esme, obviously, but I could have come up with something else. Now it felt like it was too late.

I wish I'd at least put his toothbrush in the toilet and then back on his sink. That would have been good. Too bad I still didn't have the key to his place, or I probably could have.

"SO, how do you feel about being an aunt?" I asked Em when she came in with takeout bags with sushi in them.

"I don't fucking know." She dumped the bags on the coffee table and groaned as she sat on the couch. Potato jumped into her lap, lured by the smell of the sushi.

"It's just… It doesn't feel real. I know it's happening, but I can't believe it's happening," I said.

We dug into the containers while Potato wailed that we wouldn't share with him.

"I'm sorry," Em said.

"For what?" I shoved a roll into my face.

"I don't know. For everything that happened between you and my brother." She shrugged one shoulder.

"It's not your fault. It's no one's fault. Well, it's Wyatt's fault. Everything is pretty much his fault."

She made a face.

"I'm just so tired of his bullshit," she said, mixing in more wasabi with her soy sauce.

"Hey, same," I said, holding my chopsticks up. She clicked hers with mine in solidarity.

Things could be worse. I could be the one knocked up instead of Gretchen. I was absolutely militant about my birth control, but accidents happened.

"Anyway, I have decided this is the force I need to finally move out. I don't care if I have to live in a box. I am getting out of my house because my mom won't stop talking about being a grandmother and I'm pretty sure she wants to turn my room into a nursery? For her grandchild?" I had to admit, that was a little weird.

"Esme is going to get her own place finally too," I said. "She knows the owner of Linley's building. You want me to see if she can find out if you could get a place there?"

Em shook her head. "No worries, I actually think my uncle is going to let me stay in one of the cabins, at least until I can save up enough to maybe put a down payment on a fixer upper." Wow, buying a house. That was a huge step.

"Nice. One of the cabins by the lake?" We'd hung out there a few times before.

"Yup. It's tiny as hell, but I'll have access to my own bathroom that I don't have to share with anyone so I don't even give a fuck."

"That's the spirit!" Things were going well for my friends and I was thrilled. Linley had her pangolin-carving man and Em was finally going to get some privacy.

"So, are you and Esme official yet?"

I couldn't help but smile. Thinking about Esme made my fingers and toes tingle.

"Yeah. We are. I can't believe that I didn't go for her before. What was wrong with me?"

"You were fucking my brother?" she suggested.

I made a face. "Oh yeah. That."

Em let me gush about Esme for as long as I wanted.

Midway through dessert—green tea mochi—Esme sent me a voice memo.

"I miss you. I can't wait to see you. The time is crawling by. I feel silly for saying that, but it's the truth. When did that happen? When did I start spending all my time thinking about you?" Her voice was soft and wistful, at odds with the sounds of the music and voices around her.

Esme sighed. "Anyway, I just had to tell you. I'll see you later, babe."

Babe. It made me feel like I was glowing from the inside when she called me that.

"Okay, that was cute as fuck, you make me sick," Em said after I'd played the message for her.

"I'm sorry?" I said.

"It's fine. I'm happy you're happy. You fucking deserve it after Wyatt." Wasn't that the truth?

"HEY," Esme said in a soft voice when I opened the door for her. Em had left hours ago, and I'd spent my time waiting for her by doing some work. Or trying to do work.

"Come here," I said, holding my arms open. She fell into my arms and her lips sought mine as Stormy rushed in to search for Potato. The two animals were basically best friends at this point. Such a relief.

"I missed you, too," I said, in between kisses and trying to get her work clothes off and give her access to remove mine.

We went right for the bedroom, both racing to see who could get the other one off first.

I won.

"I brought something special with me," Esme said, after she'd come down from her orgasm.

"Ohhh, what's that?" I asked.

"Wait here," she said, giving me a wicked kiss.

When she came back, she had something in both hands that she held up for me to see.

"Oh hell yes," I said as I looked over the strap-on.

"I figured since we talked about it, you might want to give it a shot." I'd never used one before, but I'd always been interested.

"Definitely," I said, and then it was an adventure to get Esme into the harness, and to make sure the dildo was attached.

"Oh fuck," I moaned as she slid inside me.

"Good girl," Esme said.

I was her girl, in every sense of the word.

After just a few thrusts, I came hard.

Esme had such a smile of satisfaction on her face that I wished I could take a mental picture to keep forever.

"You like?" Esme asked.

"Yes. Very much. Let's do that again."

Esme raised one eyebrow. "Do you want to give it a shot?" I hadn't thought about that, but once I did, I definitely, definitely wanted to do that.

"I'm doing all kinds of things with you," I said, sitting up and kissing her.

"I like the kinds of things we do," she said. "I'm so happy you came into the bar."

Remembering how we'd started hanging out made me think of Wyatt and my plan. I was so sick of thinking about that.

"Come on," I said. "Show me how to use this thing."

AFTER OUR ADVENTURES with the strap-on, we decided sleep was important and we had the whole next day to fuck, so we called it a night and went to bed. Esme had also brought some clothes to keep at my place, as well as a toothbrush and other things she'd need. I couldn't stop being thrilled whenever I went into the bathroom and saw her stuff on the sink next to mine.

Everything was wonderful, but there was that tiny voice that reminded me over and over again about my plan. I hoped that someday I'd be able to forget it like I forgot when I was supposed to pay my taxes.

I could hope.

Chapter Fourteen

Esme and I slept in the next morning, but were awoken by a dog that needed to go out and a cat who decided he needed to be fed.

"I'll deal with the dog, you deal with the cat," Esme said in a tired voice.

"Deal."

Once the pets were handled, we got back into bed to snuggle.

"How do you feel about quiche for breakfast?" I asked.

"I feel great about quiche for breakfast. I feel even better about you for breakfast," she said, and before I could react, she was under the covers.

I helped her pull down my shorts and then her tongue was on me and I was treated to a sweet and slow orgasm that unfurled slowly and gently before rocking me completely and leaving me breathless.

I pulled back the blankets and Esme's head popped up.

"That's a great way to wake up. Much better than an alarm," I said. My entire body tingled. "I'm going to get the quiche started. Do you want some coffee?" It seemed only fair that I'd make her breakfast after she made me an orgasm.

Esme pulled herself up next to me and flopped on her back.

"Sounds perfect."

∽

I TOOK LONGER to make breakfast when she came out and kept trying to distract me, but eventually we got everything on plates and had it in bed while fighting off the dog and the cat from trying to sneak bites.

"So I love hanging out with you here, but I was thinking maybe we could go out for a hike today? And get some lunch somewhere?" she said.

I was absolutely on board with that plan, so we packed some snacks and water and sunblock and loaded up Stormy in Esme's truck and headed north to a cluster of small mountains that could be hiked pretty easily and had phenomenal views. Stormy lost her freaking mind when we got out of the car and headed into the woods, practically pulling the leash out of Esme's hand.

"This is so nice," I said, when we stepped beneath the cool shade of the trees. For the first bit of the hike, you could still hear the noises from the road, but soon they faded into rustling leaves, birds, and other critters scurrying around in the underbrush.

Esme and Stormy took the lead, naturally, and I fumbled on behind. I wasn't going to tell Esme that I couldn't remember the last time I had actually hiked an actual mountain.

"How are you doing?" Esme asked, looking back. I put my hands on my knees and panted. "Good, great."

"We can slow down."

I waved her off. "No, I'm fine," I wheezed.

She didn't look like she believed me.

Once we were well on our way, Esme let Stormy off the leash, and she'd run up ahead and then back to check on us and then back out.

Esme definitely slowed down and I was better able to keep up.

"You want to take a break?" she asked when we reached a little stream that ran through the trail.

"Sounds good," I said, and tried to hide my grimace when I sat down on a rock. Oh, I was going to be sore tomorrow.

Esme shared her water with me and I pulled out the snacks. We traded the bags back and forth in silence. We'd walked for long periods without talking, but it wasn't awkward. It was peaceful.

Stormy also got treats before running off to chase a squirrel. A few people passed us, either coming down or going up the mountain. Esme and I started a game trying to guess what was in their packs.

"Well, I hope she has a spare pair of shoes, because she's going to need them," Esme said, as we watched one woman trudge past us up the mountain wearing flip flops and carrying a designer bag instead of a pack. "I also hope she's got water in that purse."

The woman had looked miserable, but the guy she was with had smiled at us and looked like he was a happy camper.

"First date, do you think?" I asked.

"Not first date, but definitely a new relationship."

I hope we don't look that mismatched, I thought.

To be fair, at least I was having a good time. That other girl was definitely suffering.

We kept going and continued to see more and more interesting people and came up with wilder and wilder items they might have in their packs.

"I'm sorry, but there's no way that guy has an entire family-size fried chicken dinner in there," I said.

"I swear I smelled chicken when he walked by," Esme said.

After what felt like days, we made it to the top at last, and I was pretty damn proud of myself.

"Celebratory selfie," Esme said, putting her arm around me and kissing me on the cheek. I smiled and she snapped the pic. Since her arms were longer than mine, I made her use my phone to take one too.

"We're pretty fucking cute together," she said, looking at the selfies. "You good if I post this?"

"Absolutely. Don't forget to tag me," I said.

We'd been official to ourselves, and to our friends and parents. But it was a whole other bucket of chicken to post about it online. Then anyone could see it, and comment.

Wyatt was going to find out, and I couldn't figure out how I felt about that.

On one hand, there was complete joy. I really did wish I could see his face when he found out. On the other, there was that little thread of guilt running through me.

Maybe he wouldn't even care. That was something I had never considered when I'd come up with this freaking plan in the first place. Sure, he had always wanted Esme, but he had Gretchen now. They were having a baby. He had other shit going on. Esme was even more out of reach than she'd ever been.

Why would he care?

"Oh, now I've done it," Esme said, laughing and showing me the celebratory comments that were rolling in. Naturally, she had more followers than I did due to her job. I tended to keep most of my social on the down low because it was tied to my professional online work. People who were hiring me to write copy for them didn't need to see me wasted off my ass and passed out on top of a pizza with cheese stuck to my face.

Not that that had ever happened to me…

I also decided to break it to my group chat, and they were similarly supportive and thrilled. Then I had to tell them all about Esme, and why I'd been hiding her, and give them all the details. Of course I gave them some details. All the nice details.

"That's enough of that," Esme said, shoving her phone back in her bag.

She took my hand and we explored the top of the mountain and took more pictures. We even saw a bald eagle and I capture a gorgeous video of it flying across the sky.

"Mountain picnic?" Esme asked, and so we laid out a light blanket I'd brought and had some more of our snacks.

The day was absolutely perfect, so the top was crawling with other humans taking pictures and soaking in the satisfaction of having scaled an entire mountain. Then there were the geniuses who didn't seem to have any self-preservation and kept getting too close to the edge to take dramatic pictures.

"I can't look anymore," I said, turning my back. "It's giving me heart palpitations."

Esme shuddered. "Sometimes I wonder how we've managed to continue as a species."

I shoved a handful of dried cherries in my mouth and tried not to think too much about it.

Stormy had fallen asleep under a tree but woke up to come get a fresh bowl of water and some kibble Esme had packed.

I was so ready for a nap, but we still had to make our way back to the truck.

"Now, they should really have something like a ski lift that takes you all the way down," Esme said, standing up and stretching her back. She held her hand out to me.

I took it and she pulled me up.

"You read my mind."

~

"WE TOTALLY FREAKING EARNED THIS," Esme said, as we both shoved fried chicken sandwiches in our faces. The trip down the mountain really hadn't been that bad, but by the time we made it to the car, I'd been ready to eat one of my hiking boots, I was so hungry. As if by fate, there just happened to be a little park with a tiny food truck next to it right near the entrance to the mountain.

I couldn't answer Esme because my mouth was full.

There was no stopping me until after I'd polished off a plate of chocolate cake with peanut butter frosting.

"That was amazing," I said, putting my fork down after licking it clean.

"Perfect," Esme said, and I realized she was gazing at me.

"Stop it, you're going to make me blush," I said. She reached out and took my hand. "I'm so glad I'm here with you."

I squeezed her hand. "I'm so glad that I'm here with you."

Louis Armstrong's version of "La Vie En Rose" played over the speakers from the food truck, and I found myself swaying along. Esme stood up from the picnic table.

"Dance with me," she said.

I looked around. "Right here?" There were a lot of people around since it was the dinner rush.

"Yeah, come on." She made the cutest little pouty face I'd ever seen in my life, and if she would have asked for a vital organ, I would have picked up the knife on my plate and start carving it out for her.

Why not?

I got up and let Esme pull me into her arms. The moment we started swaying, I stopped thinking about who was watching. There was only the two of us, dancing next to a food truck.

"I'm really sorry if I'm sweaty," I said. I'd like to see the person who could complete a hike without sweating buckets.

"I've been sweaty with you before, Paige. Remember?" she

whispered in my ear. Oh yes, I did remember. And I couldn't wait to get her back to my place so we could continue.

Stormy barked at us from the truck.

"I think someone is jealous," I said.

"She's just mad she has to share now. It's fine, she'll get extra treats later," she said.

Esme and I kept dancing until Stormy really started making a fuss and we got back in the truck and gave her attention.

"We should probably get back anyway," Esme said. "What did you want to do for dinner? We could stop and get something, or maybe, I could cook for you."

I leaned closer to her, watching her hair blow in the breeze of the open window. Stormy snoozed contentedly in the backseat. If only we had Potato, and the fish, the gang would be all here.

"I'd love to have you cook for me," I said. "I will warn you, I get a little territorial about my kitchen, but I'll try and tone it down for you." I trusted someone like Linley, for instance, to treat my kitchen right, but other people not so much.

"What could I possibly do in your kitchen that would harm it?" she asked.

"Wyatt set spaghetti on fire. I didn't even know that was possible." That boy was so pretty, but about as sharp as a doorknob.

Esme reached out to take my hand and kiss the back of it. "I promise not to set any spaghetti on fire."

"Thank you. I appreciate that."

I couldn't stop smiling.

"YOU GO RELAX and let me handle this," Esme said, when I tried to sneak into the kitchen to see how the dinner progress was going.

Inspired by my story, she'd decided to make spaghetti, but with her own sauce recipe and fresh meatballs, and I was trying not to stress.

Disgruntled, I went into the living room as she rolled up more meatballs and set them on a baking sheet.

I was just about to turn on the TV when a message came through on one of my social media pages.

Wyatt.

I probably shouldn't read it, but that didn't stop me from clicking on it.

I give it a week. She'll get tired of you not satisfying her.

My face got so hot that I started sweating.

Oh *fuck him*.

I shouldn't respond. *I shouldn't respond.*

"What's that?" Esme said from over my shoulder. I hadn't noticed that she'd left the kitchen and was peering over my shoulder.

"Nothing," I said, closing the message without deleting it.

I felt sick. There was no way I could eat anything now.

"Hey, are you okay? What was that?" she asked.

"Wyatt," I said as tears started to slide down my cheeks. Fucking hell. Why couldn't he just leave me alone?

Esme went to turn off the simmering sauce so it wouldn't boil over and came to sit with me on the couch.

"What did he say?"

"Nothing." I didn't want her to know. It was too embarrassing.

"You can tell me. I've had awful exes too." She rubbed my shoulder and looked at me with such open compassion that it made me want to cry harder.

"He's just a terrible person and I loved him. What does that say about me?" I asked.

I didn't mean to tell her that. I didn't mean to tell *anyone* that.

"It doesn't say anything. It's not your fault. You're not responsible for anything he does, and you don't deserve anything he does," she said.

Esme hugged me for a long time.

"Why are you so good to me?" I whispered.

"Because I think I'm falling in love with you," she whispered back.

I sat back and stared at her. "Wait, are you serious?"

"Yeah," she said. "I am."

"Oh. Wow." This was a lot to process.

"You don't have to say anything right now," she said. "I just wanted to share with you how I feel."

Several moments of silence passed between us as we both tried to figure out where to go from here.

She was waiting for me to say something, but there was only one thing to say: the truth.

"I'm falling in love with you too," I said, and she smiled so brightly, I thought her cheeks would crack.

"Really?"

"Really." She kissed me and I pushed Wyatt aside. He didn't get to have this. He didn't get to have me, or my time, or my space. I wouldn't let him ruin this.

THE SPAGHETTI WAS SERVED LATER than intended, but it was absolutely worth the wait.

"Okay, I'm going to need this recipe," I said as I shoved an entire meatball in my mouth. Her sauce was perfect, the meatballs were perfect, and the pasta was done just right. Esme Bell was a spaghetti savant.

"Thank you, thank you," she said, taking a little bow.

She'd even made Stormy a tiny plate with one tiny meatball of her own.

Potato had come to sniff my plate but had been uninterested a moment later. All the more for me.

"I'm looking at taking a few days off next month and I was thinking maybe we could go somewhere," Esme said. "How do you feel about road trips?"

"I feel awesome about road trips." I also felt awesome about staying in hotels with massive beds and ordering room service.

"How about we each come up with some ideas and then we can present them and vote on it," she suggested.

"Deal. But I'm going to win."

She raised an eyebrow. "Oh, you really think so?"

I pointed my fork at her. "I know so."

She just stuck her tongue out at me.

"That's very mature behavior for a bartender."

"At least I'm not puking into someone else's beer glass while they're in the bathroom," she said. I almost gagged. There was no doubt that this was something that had definitely happened at least once.

"Please don't tell me those kinds of stories when I'm eating," I said. "Or I might be forced to take extreme measures."

Her eyes went wide.

"What kind of extreme measures?" she said.

I narrowed my eyes. "You'll find out."

"Ohhhh, I'm scared," she said.

Stormy put her head on Esme's lap to beg for another meatball.

"No, my love, you can't have another one." This caused Stormy to start wailing dramatically, which made Potato get a case of the zoomies and start doing laps around the house.

"Maybe you should just give her a meatball," I said over Stormy's wailing.

Esme shook her head. "Give in to her tantrums and she'll know that she can make a fuss and get her way." That made sense. If I gave into every one of Potato's whims, he would weigh so much more and probably have broken a lot more things.

"She'll stop," Esme said as Stormy continued to scream, looking over at us to judge our reactions.

"She's really putting on a show," Esme said. "I promise she's not normally this bad."

We finished our dinner with an unhappy dog, but said unhappy dog got distracted by the cat and we were able to eat our dessert in peace. Esme found a box of brownie mix that I didn't remember buying and made those topped with ice cream and sprinkles.

"Sexy sundaes," she said, putting whipped cream on hers.

"What makes them sexy?" I asked.

"They're sexy because I'm having them with you and you're sexy."

My face went red, and I almost dropped the sundae dish.

"You're so cute," Esme said, putting down her bowl. "I could just eat you up."

She put her hands on my waist and helped me hop up on the counter, leaning in to kiss me.

"You ate me this morning."

"Mmmm, please remind me," she said, nipping at my lower lip.

The ice cream was forgotten as we kissed. Esme was much sweeter anyway.

"Now it's my turn to have you for dessert," I said, pushing her back toward the bedroom.

"Oh is it?" she asked, giving me a coy smile.

"Yes."

∽

"I THINK we left the ice cream on the counter," Esme said a while later after I'd made her come twice.

"Oh well," I said. "The sacrifice was worth it."

Esme sat up and listened. "It's too quiet."

Oh no.

She bolted out of bed and ran into the kitchen to find Stormy attempting to get to the ice cream container. Thankfully, she hadn't been able to reach it, because I didn't think ice cream was good for dogs.

"Oops," I said, putting the ice cream in the trash.

"No harm done. We just need to be more careful. At least she didn't go for the brownies, or we would be off to the emergency vet right now."

Stormy looked at both of us with wide, innocent eyes.

"I'm not buying it," Esme said to Stormy.

"We should probably clean up anyway," I said, and we put our robes on before going back to deal with the mess and making sure the rest of the house didn't have anything else that Stormy could get into. The house was already Potato-proof, but it never hurt to make sure.

"We still have brownies," I said, so we brought those to the couch and cuddled while watching a few episodes of an old show from the 90s.

Everything was almost perfect. I had the girl I was falling in love with in my arms, the most amazing girl that I couldn't even believe had looked at me, let alone gotten naked and shared so much with me. My cat had a playmate, my bills were paid, and my mom wasn't contacting me to fix a crisis.

If it weren't for the Wyatt bullshit, my world would be ideal.

But if I hadn't decided to get back at Wyatt, would I have

even approached Esme? I didn't know the answer to that question, and I didn't like that I didn't know.

"I'M SO glad your ex made me bring you that drink," Esme said later as we lay in bed together. Neither of us wanted to go to sleep. I couldn't stop running my hands through her hair.

"Can you not remind me of him?" I asked. "Sorry, that was harsh. But I don't want to think about him."

"I'm sorry," she said softly. "I think we would have gotten together eventually. I wouldn't have let you walk around being so cute without asking you out at some point."

I didn't know if that was true either.

"I have to tell you something," I whispered.

She sat up and turned the light on. "What is it?"

"Remember when we first started hanging out?" My entire body was shaking.

"Yeah," Esme said.

"Well, I first went after you because… because…" I couldn't seem to get the words out. I took a breath. "Because I was trying to get back at Wyatt. He's had this huge fucking thing for you for years, so I thought that if I could get with you, then I could rub it in his face and I know how terrible that sounds, but I'm so sorry, and I couldn't keep it inside anymore." The words came out of my mouth so quickly that I wasn't sure if Esme even understood me.

I waited for her reaction.

"You talked with me to get back at him," she said slowly, looking down at the blankets.

"Yes," I said, and then I started to cry. "I'm sorry."

Esme was silent for a long time. What felt like hours.

"Okay. That's… that's a lot to think about, Paige. When

did things change for you? Or are you still trying to get back at him?"

"No!" I tried to reach for her hand. "I'm not trying to get back at him. I forgot all about him after that first night you stayed here."

She got out of bed and stood up. "You slept with me to get back at him and only realized you had real feelings for me after?"

The tears came harder now. I never should have said anything. Linley was right.

"I'm sorry. It was such a fucking bad idea. I never meant to hurt you," I said.

Esme put her hand up. "I think I need to go home and think about this for a little while. I don't... I can't be here right now."

I wanted to scream, I wanted to grab her and beg her to stay. I wanted to throw myself in front of her truck so she'd have to run over me if she wanted to leave.

I didn't do any of that. Instead, I sat in bed and cried as she put her clothes on and gathered up Stormy and left.

Her truck roared in the quiet night as she pulled out of the driveway, and I sat there and cried. Potato jumped up on the bed, confused at what was going on.

"I fucked it up, Potato. I fucked everything up."

Chapter Fifteen

I GOT ABOUT zero sleep that night. I couldn't stop thinking about the look on Esme's face when I told her. All I wanted to do was get in my car and go to her dad's house and beg her to talk to me. I'd composed at least a hundred different text messages to her in my head, and I'd even written out and deleted a dozen of them.

In the end, there was nothing I could say that would make it better. I'd done a shitty thing. She'd asked for time to process, and I was going to give it to her.

There was nothing to do for me except wait, and hope, and sit in my misery.

"THE BALL IS IN HER COURT," Linley said, when I went to confess what I'd told Esme the night before.

"I know. I just... I just wish there was something I could do. Some way to take it back," I said.

Linley had pushed a plate of chocolate chip oatmeal cookies at me, but I couldn't eat any of them. Things were really bad if I couldn't stomach Linley's cookies.

"I'd give her another day and maybe send a check-in text," she said, washing her hands of flour in the sink. I'd come after the bakery was closed so I hadn't had to see anyone. I'd worked from home today, too.

Couldn't deal with seeing too many people. I didn't want anyone to see the shame that was written all over my face. I couldn't even tell Em.

"I'm sorry," Linley said, giving me a hug. She didn't need to tell me I'd been an ass because I knew. She didn't need to say "I told you so" because I knew.

"Enough about me and my fuckups, how is your handsome pangolin carver?" Linley tried to hide a smile, but she couldn't.

"He's wonderful. I know we were planning on having dinner this weekend, but I can put it off," she said.

"No, it's fine. It'll take my mind off things. Hopefully I'll be less wallowy by then."

"I'll take you even if you're wallowy," she said.

I took a shuddering breath and felt myself start to cry again. "I have a feeling that I'm going to be wallowy for a while, if that's okay."

Linley handed me a paper towel. "You really liked her, I could tell. It was all over your face."

"I'm falling in love with her," I whispered. "I can't handle having my heart broken again." I didn't think I'd survive it. My heart had already been so damn fragile. Could it break permanently? I didn't want to know the answer.

I SENT Esme a text that night as I sat in my car in the driveway after getting back from seeing Linley. I knew I should have waited, but I couldn't stand the silence.

I'm so sorry. I just needed you to know that.

There was no answer, so I went inside to make myself something to eat. I'd barely had anything all day, and even though I was still completely wrecked about Esme, I had to eat something. Luckily, I had a few frozen meals stashed for such occasions and I pulled out a chicken and rice dinner to shove in the microwave. While it was cooking, I opened a package I'd received: a wooden puzzle in the shape of an anatomical heart. I'd gotten it for Esme. Looking at it made me feel sick, so I shoved it under the couch.

Potato would not stop following me around and crying, even though he'd been fed, his litter was clean, and there was nothing else wrong.

"Are you looking for your friend? Do you miss Stormy?" I asked, leaning down to pet him.

"I miss her, and her owner too." A single tear fell on Potato's fur, and I wiped it away.

A rumbling sound made me look up as the microwaved dinged, announcing that my food was ready.

Ignoring the food, I ran to the door.

Esme's truck was in my driveway. It was still light enough out that I could see her sitting in the driver's seat, as if she was deciding what to do next.

I waited.

She took a breath and got out of the truck. Stormy wasn't with her.

I could barely breath as Esme stepped toward the door and knocked.

To not appear too eager, I waited a few seconds before I opened it.

"Hi," I said, unable to stop crying again. How many tears could one human body produce? I'd had to chug so much water today so I didn't get dehydrated.

"Hi," she said, and it wasn't lost on me that the area around her eyes was puffy and red.

"Hi," I said again and realized that I'd already said that.

"Can I come in?" she asked.

"Yes, of course." I moved to let her in. "Do you want to sit down?"

"Sure," she said, and we took seats on the couch with some space between us. I didn't want to jump all over her or presume anything. Her face was closed, and I could not get a read on how this was going to go.

The silence was so heavy, I couldn't get enough air into my lungs. Potato ran over and jumped in Esme's lap. She said hello and started petting him, so I took that as a positive sign.

"Okay, so, I'm still not really sure what I want to say. I really didn't think you were the kind of person who would do something like that, Paige. I didn't think you'd use someone like that for something so petty. I understand that Wyatt is a huge asshole, but you didn't have to do that. I'm not against getting back at an ex, but using me to do it? Not okay," she said.

She was right. There was nothing I could say to that, because it was true.

She took a deep breath. "With that said, I still think we have something good here, and I'm not going to throw it away that quickly. It's going to take some time to build back that trust, but I'm willing to take that risk."

Our eyes met and I sucked in a jagged breath.

"Paige?" she asked. I realized I needed to respond.

"Yes. I, yes, I want to work on this with you. I'm just so sorry, Esme. There's no excuse or justification," I said.

Potato purred loudly, oblivious to the seriousness of the conversation.

"No, there isn't, but I understand where you were coming from. I just wish you would have snuck into his house and moved all of his furniture a centimeter a day until nothing was in the same place and he thought his house was haunted by furniture-moving ghosts."

She smiled and it was like the tension cracked.

"Where were you when I was making revenge plans? That would have been so much better," I said.

Esme leaned closer. "Next time run your revenge plots by me. I may look sweet, but I can be petty."

"I like petty," I said.

I felt my face make a smile for the first time in twenty-four hours.

My microwave beeped angrily, reminding me that my dinner had been sitting in there and was probably cold again.

"Do you want some dinner? I can make you something." I'd make her anything she wanted.

Esme thought about that for a moment. "Yeah, that would be great."

ESME SEEMED to want some space, so I gave it to her. I didn't snuggle close to her on the couch, I didn't put my arms around her or pull her in for a kiss. I'd let her decide what she was comfortable with.

She did keep me company as I whipped together a quick dinner of chicken and rice and green beans after I'd tossed the forgotten microwave meal. The food wasn't fancy, but it did the trick.

Being with her was so easy and relaxing that all the tension in my body evaporated in her presence.

"I don't have any ice cream, but I do have some chocolate strawberries in the back of the freezer," I said.

She stretched her arms over her head and yawned. "Sounds perfect. Sorry, I didn't get a lot of sleep. I was doing a lot of thinking."

It was like a curtain had been pulled across a window with the sun shining outside. A reminder of what I'd done, and that Esme was only here because she was willing to give me another chance.

My stomach twisted with guilt.

"Hey, I know that you did a shitty thing, but I don't want you to get too down about yourself. We all make mistakes. God knows I've made many," she said. Her hand rested on my arm and all I wanted was to give her a hug.

I leaned in and she let me, wrapping her arms around me.

"I missed you. I know it was only a short time, but I didn't like it. At all. I'm going to do whatever I can not to mess up like that again," I said.

Esme pulled back and looked me deep in the eyes. "You'll mess up. I'll mess up. It's how we deal with those mess ups that matters. It's how we move forward." She really was good at advice.

"Have you ever thought about being a therapist? You'd be really good at it," I said.

Esme shrugged. "I don't know about that. I like my job. I like what I do. I'm happy at the bar. Of course, I have other things I want to do, like with my blog and stuff, but I guess I just wasn't born with too much career ambition." She laughed, but I could tell that this was a sensitive subject for her. I'd heard similar things when I hadn't gone to grad school or "lived up to my potential" whatever that meant.

"You can sit with me in the low-career ambition corner," I said. That made her smile.

"It's a good place to be. We have snacks and drinks."

Speaking of that, I got the strawberries out of the freezer to thaw a little before we devoured them.

"If you want to stay, you can. I can always crash on the couch and give you the bed. Or you can go home. No pressure," I said, as it got later, and Esme's yawns got more frequent.

"It's okay. I think I'll go home because I didn't bring Stormy. She misses you, by the way. Or she misses Potato. She put up a huge fuss and was looking all over the house for something or someone."

"Potato has been upset too. I'll have to bring him with me when you move into your new place." This was assuming we didn't crash and burn before then.

"Speaking of my new place, I'm going to see two of the available units this weekend. Do you want to come with me?" That was a good sign. She wanted my input on her apartment.

"I'd love to," I said, and she held a strawberry out for me to take a bite. I did, licking chocolate off my lips.

Esme giggled. "You have chocolate all over your face."

I raised an eyebrow. "Why don't you help me clean it off?" I hoped I wasn't pushing her too far.

Esme only hesitated for a moment before she leaned forward and kissed the side of my mouth, and I felt the warm lick of her tongue. My chin was next, and then the opposite corner. She hesitated just before truly meeting my lips in a kiss that was both sweet and slow. Like melted chocolate.

I kissed her back, leaning into her and wrapping my hands around her back, one hand in her hair.

"I missed you too," she whispered. "I really should go home, though."

"I know," I said, in between kisses. "But I don't want you to."

"I don't want to go." Her hands drifted from my shoulders and downward, until they were pushing under my shirt.

"Then don't go," I said through a gasp as she pushed my shirt higher.

She groaned and removed her hands.

"No, I should go." She got up from the couch and put her

hands up as if to stop me from coming after her. My entire body throbbed with need.

"I'm not above begging you to stay. Or showing you my boobs to get you to stay," I said, starting to lift my shirt.

"No, don't." Esme slapped her hand over her eyes.

"Don't show you my boobs? Okay then." I pushed my shirt back down and she peeked between her fingers.

"You're too irresistible for your own good, Paige."

No one had called me irresistible before. I guess I *could* be a seducer.

We stared at each other, heat crackling between us. It would be so simple to get off the couch and go to her.

I didn't. I literally sat on my hands to keep from reaching for Esme.

"I'm going," she said, but she wasn't moving.

I waited.

What seemed like hours later, she closed her eyes, took a breath, and then opened her eyes and rushed toward the door.

"Thanks for dinner, I'll let you know when I get home, bye," she said in a rush before slamming the door.

I dashed to the window and watched her throw herself in her truck and get out of my driveway as if a murderer was chasing her.

About ten minutes later I got a text message from her.

I'm sorry I ran out. It was the only way to make sure I left and didn't go back and take all of your clothes off.

I moaned when I read it.

You could have. I would have let you. I wanted you to.

I wasn't good at denying myself that kind of pleasure. More orgasms were always better in my book.

I wanted to. Fuck, I wanted to. I called in sick

today, but I have to work tomorrow, but I'll come over after with Stormy. Okay?

Fuck. Yes. That was more than okay, and I told her so.

I'd fucked up, but we were on the right track again, and I was never, ever, going to hurt her like that again.

Chapter Sixteen

"IT'S NICE?" I said as Esme, Chuck, the building owner, and me walked around the empty apartment. It was shiny and new like Linley's place. In fact, her place was right across the hall. I guess I just couldn't picture Esme living here. Couldn't see Stormy sleeping in a dog bed by the door. It just wasn't her, and I couldn't put my finger on why.

"You said the same thing about the other place," Esme pointed out. I wasn't trying to be a pain, but I didn't want to lie either.

"I think it's because it's hard for me to picture it without furniture or anything in it," I said. "Sorry."

Esme sighed and ran her hand down the granite countertop.

"Why don't I give you two a minute?" Chuck said, checking a new message on his phone. "I'll be right outside." He started to make a call and stepped into the hallway, shutting the front door behind him.

"Why don't you like either of these places?" Esme asked, as soon as the door closed.

"I don't know. They just don't seem like you. I can't explain it. But it's not my decision, it's yours, and I'll support you no matter what. It's a great building. Linley loves it here." I was going to suck it up and be there for her. It would be great to finally have a place that was hers that we could stay at without worrying about waking up her dad.

Esme looked around and crossed her arms. "I don't know. I'm not getting the right vibe. You're right. There's something off."

"It's probably just because it's empty," I said.

Esme sighed again. "I mean, I shouldn't be so picky. Right now I'm sharing a bathroom with my father. The rent is affordable, and Chuck is giving me a good deal. I know he's not going to fuck me over."

She sat right down on the floor, crossing her legs. I joined her.

"You could always just move in with me," I said, laughing. "Then Stormy and Potato could hang out all the time."

She laughed for a minute, and then stopped. "Wait, are you serious? You want me to move in with you?"

I didn't think I was serious when I said it, but now that I pictured it? Yeah, I was serious.

"Yes. I want you to move in with me," I said.

Esme's eyes went wide. "We literally just started dating and had our first fight. Doesn't that seem way too soon?"

I lifted one shoulder. "Probably. But I've never been one to go by normal timelines for things. Once I'm in, I'm all in." I leaned forward, putting my hands on her shins. "I'm all in with you, Esme."

She blinked a few times and shook her head. "Can I think about it?"

"Of course. I don't expect you to be as impulsive as me. One of us has to be the voice of reason." I'd been in relationships with other impulsive people, and they always ended in complete unmitigated disaster.

She exhaled, as if she was relieved. "Now I'm thinking about it."

Esme scooted her back up against the bar and I moved so our shoulders touched and leaned my head onto her shoulder.

"I like the idea of coming home to you, Paige. Seeing you on the couch with your laptop and your glasses. Watching you make dinner. Waking up to you every morning. Plus, you have a great yard for a dog."

That was true. This building didn't have much of a yard, so there was no place for Stormy to go.

"See? I can come up with good plans." I hadn't been referencing my previous awful plan, but I winced when I remembered.

Esme put her arm around me.

"It is a good plan. My dad is going to wonder what the hell I'm thinking," she said.

I sat up. "Wait, does that mean you're saying yes? I thought you wanted to think about it."

She met my eyes and smiled slowly. "I did think about it. And I decided. I would love to move in with you, Paige." She reached for me and our lips met.

"I promise I'll get rid of a bunch of my crap. And we can get new sheets. And if you hate my curtains, we can get new ones," I said in a rush, but Esme just quieted me with a kiss.

We kissed for so long that we didn't break apart until Chuck knocked on the door and walked back in to find us slightly disheveled.

Both of us got to our feet, a little embarrassed.

"So, thanks for the offer, Chuck, it seriously means a lot. But I think I'm going to make other arrangements for right now." Esme took my hand and squeezed it and I felt so happy that I wouldn't have been surprised if I was actually glowing.

Chuck didn't seem upset, and we traded banter back and forth as he locked up the unit again and led us out to the front.

"Holy shit, we're moving in together," I said, when we got into Esme's truck.

"Yeah. We are. What's your mom going to say?" she asked.

"Oh, she's definitely going to need to meet you officially now. I'm sorry in advance." I'd definitely have to have a talk with her about not hitting up my girlfriend to join her down-line in her "business." I'd been down that road before and it wasn't pretty.

"Dad wants you to come over for dinner next week, by the way. I'll tell him about moving in together before then, though. I'm not sure how he's going to take it, but he knows who you are. He likes you. Says you're always nice to him when you're at the store." It was so strange, that I'd had hundreds of interactions with her father, but now everything was different because I was dating his daughter.

"Okay. I think I can handle that," I said. Esme grabbed my hand.

"We'll deal with our parents together, Paige. We've got this."

I WENT to meet Gray with Linley, and invited Esme along because I figured why not just double? He was just as sweet as I remembered, and he was absolutely head over heels for Linley. I could appreciate his good taste.

Esme kept us all entertained with her bartender stories, and she and Gray got in a deep conversation about art that was way over my head.

It was a lovely evening, and Esme came back to stay at my place with Stormy. She and Potato were the bestest of friends now, so having Esme move in just made sense. It was only fair to our pets.

"You'll have to tell me what you absolutely hate," I said as we crashed on the couch that night.

"I don't hate anything in here," Esme said. "I like your stuff. Maybe we can just put some of it away."

I narrowed my eyes.

"So, you don't like all of my stuff," I said.

Esme shook her head. "No, no, I like your stuff. There's just a lot of it. Everywhere."

I glared and then started laughing when I couldn't keep up the facade.

"Esme, it's fine. I know I have a lot of shit, and I know I need to organize things better. There's plenty of room in the basement for stuff. I want you to feel like this place is yours too. Not that you're just visiting, or a guest. This is going to be your place," I said.

We'd already agreed that Esme and I would split expenses, which was great for me, since I'd be able to pay a little more each month toward my student loan debt. Asking Esme to move in with me was the most fiscally responsible thing I'd ever done.

~

"YOU ASKED HER TO *WHAT?*" my mom screeched as we sat at the table eating dinner. I'd gotten her another lasagna in hopes of softening the news.

"She's moving in with me. Next week. And her dog," I said. We'd already ordered some fencing to enclose part of the yard for Stormy.

Mom sat there and stared at me, open-mouthed.

"Paige, you've always been impulsive when it came to love, but this is a whole other level. Are you sure about this?" I poked my fork into my piece of lasagna.

"Yes, I'm sure. I can't explain how I know it's right, but it's right," I said.

Mom let out a tense breath. "You thought it was right all those other times, too," she said gently. Okay, that was fair, but I couldn't make her understand that this was different. Esme was different. Now that I had distance from my relationship with Wyatt, I saw all the cracks that had been there the whole time. I saw the problems that I'd ignored. I saw how incompatible we were. Hindsight hurt like a bitch.

"I love her," I said, and I hadn't even known I was going to say it before the words came out of my mouth. They rang through my bones with truth. I loved Esme. Really, and truly.

"Oh, Paige. I love you and I know she's a nice girl, and I'll support you in what you want to do, but I'm just going to have some reservations."

I nodded. "That's fair. I think you should meet her, though. We're having dinner with her dad next week."

"Would you mind if I tagged along? I've always liked Butch. He helps me pick out the perfect avocados." The way that my mom said the last part was weird. As if picking out avocados wasn't about picking out avocados.

Did my mom have a thing for Esme's dad? That was too horrifying to contemplate right now.

"Okay," I said, hoping to change the subject.

Fortunately, Mom started chattering about other things, and I was left to let my mind wander.

I loved Esme. Holy shit.

I loved her and I didn't know if I should tell her.

"HOW DID IT GO?" Esme asked, looking up from her book as I walked in from having dinner with my mom.

"Exhausting," I said, falling onto the couch next to her.

Stormy was asleep on the floor next to the dog bed that Potato was curled up in the center off. Typical.

"But she was okay with everything?"

I closed my eyes and leaned my head back. I needed a massage.

"Yeah, pretty much. She thinks we're rushing, but what else is new?"

Oh, by the way, I am completely in love with you, just wanted you to know, I thought.

I mean, it wasn't completely out of left field that I loved her. I'd known I was falling before. But we had literally just had big drama and had made a huge decision to move in together. Was it too much too soon? Would I freak her out?

"What is it?" she asked. I'd been silent, thinking about the fact that I loved her. Oops.

"Nothing," I said. Nothing except those three words.

"Okay," she said, but I could tell she was suspicious. "How about a drink?"

"That sounds perfect."

Esme went to the kitchen and did her mixology magic and came back with a glass of… something. One of her favorite things was making a drink and not telling me what it was and having me do a taste test.

"You're so lucky I love you," I said as I prepared to take a sip.

"What?" she asked, and I had to fumble to not drop the glass, splashing a little bit of the reddish liquid on the floor.

"Shit!" I slammed the drink down on the coffee table, causing even more of a mess.

"What did you say?" Esme said, staring at me.

"Nothing, I said nothing!" I yelled. Why was I yelling?

"Did you say you loved me?" she asked.

I panicked, looking for the exits. Esme was between me and

the front door. Maybe I could head out the back and throw myself through the screen on the porch.

"Paige," Esme said, getting my focus back. My heart pounded as if it too was trying to escape.

"What?" I asked.

"Did you say you loved me?" Guess now was as good a time as any?

"Yes?" I said, bracing for her reaction.

"Okay," she said, taking a few steps toward me. I froze, waiting for what she'd say next. It would change everything.

"That's good, because I love you too," she said.

I closed my eyes and took a shaky breath. When I opened them again, she was still there, standing in front of me with a massive smile on her face. As if she'd just won the lottery.

"You do?" I asked, my voice squeaking.

"Yeah, I do." She put her arms around me, and even though my hands were still wet and sticky from spilling the drink, I wrapped myself around her, our lips meeting for a kiss that felt like coming home.

"I love you," she said, pulling back. "I was just waiting to tell you. I thought with the moving in and everything else, it might be too much."

I stared at her. "I thought the same thing."

She laughed. "Guess you're rubbing off on me, Paige."

"I have no idea if that's a good thing or not."

She kissed the tip of my nose. "It's a very good thing. You're a very good thing. The best thing."

I kissed her again, and I didn't know if it was possible to survive this level of happiness. I had the most beautiful, sexy, funny, sweet girl in my arms, and she loved me back and was moving in with me. How in the hell had that happened?

She'd been right here the whole time, but maybe this was how it was meant to happen. We were right, now.

"I hope you're ready for this," Esme said.

"I am," I said, completely confident. "I'm ready for husky fur everywhere, and you coming home late from work, and fighting over how many pillows we have on the bed. I'm ready for all of it."

"Wait, hold on. You're ready for the pillow conversation?" Her eyebrows lifted, as if she doubted me.

"Yes. As long as the conversation is 'yes, Paige can have as many pillows as she wants.'"

Esme sighed. "No. That's not how a discussion works."

"But it's how I *want* the discussion to work," I whined.

Esme laughed. "Living together is going to go extremely well. I don't foresee any conflicts whatsoever."

"Okay, I can compromise on pillows, if you can compromise on letting me handle my own haircare."

Esme made a little pained sound. "Don't you want to have nicer hair?"

"Don't you want to have a more comfortable and supported sleeping experience?" I fired back.

"We are at an impasse," she said.

"So be it."

Stormy woke up and came over to see what was happening, and Potato followed.

"We're not fighting," I reassured the animals. "We're fine. We're just having a discussion."

They didn't look convinced.

"Mama Paige just thinks she needs too many pillows," Esme said, petting Stormy.

"Enough about my pillows!" I said.

Esme stood up and gave me a look, and the air instantly changed and got hotter. "I will admit, sometimes those pillows can come in handy."

"Yeah?" I said.

"Yeah. Let me show you something new," she said, walking back toward the bedroom.

"Esme, have you been looking up adult content on the internet?" I said with faux shock.

"No, never. My mind is just dirty enough that I think of these things all on my own."

I whimpered as she pushed the bedroom door open.

"Now let's get those clothes off," she said.

"FUCK, I LOVE YOU," I said, about a half hour later. Esme lay next to me, sweaty and satisfied.

"I love you, Paige. I don't care how we started. I only care that we're here now, and I get to be with you and build a future with you."

I wrapped myself around her and relished the feel of her skin on mine.

Everything I'd gone through with past relationships had been worth it to get this. To have her.

"As long as our future includes pillows and mystery drinks and beach days and sharing onion rings and mind-blowing sex," I said.

"I think we can make that happen," Esme said, pushing my hair back.

"Good," I said, closing my eyes.

Epilogue

"I HAVE GOT to take these shoes off," I said, sitting down next to Esme and slipping off the rose gold shoes that matched my bridesmaid's dress. The shoes had been fine when I bought them for Linley's wedding a few months ago, but standing and dancing my ass off for hours was going to take a toll, no matter what I had on my feet.

"Poor Paige. I'll give you a foot massage later," Esme said. She was looking hot as hell in a backless black dress that showed off her new tattoos. It wasn't my imagination that more than a few of the wedding guests had been checking her out the whole evening. That happened all the time, and I'd gotten used to it in the past year and a half we'd been together.

"I can't tell who's happier, Linley or her mom," I said, leaning against Esme.

"I'm going with Martha. I thought she was going to faint when they finally said 'I do.'"

I laughed. "I know! Now she'll start the countdown for grandbabies." Poor Linley was never going to hear the end of it until she produced an heir to the Sweet's bakery empire.

"Yes, and we know *nothing* about that kind of pressure,"

Esme said, rolling her eyes. Between my mom and her dad, we had our own set of parental pressures to deal with. After some initial reluctance, my mom had fallen so in love with Esme, she'd become best friends with Butch. Personally, I thought they were banging on the side, but Esme said she didn't want to even think about that, so I didn't bring it up anymore.

Esme kept randomly twitching and it was getting distracting. I didn't know why she was being so jumpy. The wedding was over, and she hadn't even been in it. Why was she so nervous?

"Oh, Linley's going to throw the bouquet," I said, as people started to gather on the dance floor and fight for it. I was prepared to sit back and watch the mayhem.

"Come on," Esme said, getting up.

I shook my head. "No way. I'm not participating in that. I don't want to lose an eye," I said.

Esme kept looking at the crowd and then back at me.

"Oh, come on, we'll stay in the back," she said. Esme was being weird about this, but whatever. If she wanted to participate, then that was fine. I was just grateful Linley didn't do the whole garter thing. Gross.

Esme and I took up residence in the back, far away from the bouquet. There was literally no way that either of us was going to get it.

"One, two, three!" Linley yelled and I waited to see the bouquet flying through the air and people bumping into each other to reach for it.

"What's happening?" I asked, as I watched Linley run over to us and shove the bouquet at me, a huge smile on her face.

I couldn't understand what was going on. What was the point of the toss if she was just going to give it to me?

"Take it," Linley said.

"Okay?" I said.

I took the bouquet and literally everyone was staring at me. What the fuck?

Someone tapped me on the shoulder and I turned to the side to see Esme down on one knee, holding out a ring box.

"Oh my god what the fuck?" I said, dropping the bouquet.

"I love you so much, Paige. You're everything to me. I can't wait to spend every day of the rest of our lives together. Will you marry me?" she said.

I was crying so hard I couldn't speak, but I was able to nod as everyone cheered and I held out a shaky hand to let Esme slip the ring on. I barely even looked at it as she swept me up in her arms and spun me around and kissed me over and over.

The DJ started playing "La Vie En Rose," and Esme set me down.

"You never said yes," Esme pointed out.

"Yes, fuck yes, I will marry the hell out of you."

We swayed back and forth for a few seconds in bliss. Everything felt like a dream.

Our parents came over to congratulate us and then it was an avalanche of people hugging us and offering their support and me yelling at Linley and everyone else for hiding this from me.

At last, I got to go back and dance with my new fiancée.

"I was so nervous about this," she said.

Everything made sense now.

"Oh, that's why you've been twitchy all day. I thought you were just nervous about the wedding or being around people or saw an ex or something," I said.

To be fair, there were definitely a few exes in attendance, but I'd been ignoring them.

"Nope. I had to stop myself from constantly checking for the ring," she said.

I looked at my hand for the first time to really check out the ring.

It was beautiful with a square sapphire and a white gold band that had a curling pattern like waves carved on it. The ring was everything I could have wanted.

"It's perfect," I said. "Wait, where did you hide the box?"

Esme winked at me. "I got a thigh holster. I'll show you later."

"Holy shit, that is the hottest thing. You could have led with that and I would have said yes," I said.

Esme threw her head back and laughed.

"I love you so much, Paige."

About Just One Week, Castleton Hearts
Book Two

Emerald Witmer is beyond pissed when her brother begs her to drive all the way across the country to pick up his girlfriend's sister from college and bring her back to Castleton, Maine. She would tell him to go *blank* himself, but then he agrees to pay her, and let's be real, she could use the money.

She's not going to think about the fact that the girl she's going to pick up, Natalie Johnson, was her best friend when they were kids until Natalie decided she'd rather hang with the cool kids and abandoned Em. Not that she's still holding a grudge or anything.

All she has to do is manage to get through one week with Natalie, and then never think about her again, but those plans go out the window when she sees Natalie and there's another feeling that is more intense than anger at what she did in the past: lust.

It's fine. All she has to do is get through one week. What happens afterwards is a problem for future Em.

What starts as an annoying chore turns into a road trip of redemption when Em realizes how much she misses having Natalie in her life, and things escalate further when they get back to Castleton, and share a kiss. Those feelings Em has been trying to ignore aren't going to be silenced. Will Em put the past in the past and let herself fall for the girl who used to be her best friend? Or will she hold onto her past hurt and reject Natalie completely?

"It's one week, Emmi, come on," my brother, Wyatt, whined. Well, Wyatt didn't exactly whine, but he was doing his best beg. He was so good-looking that he didn't have to do it very often. Things mostly just fell in his lap. Since I was his sister, I was completely immune to any of his charms.

"No, I can't do it." I knew I was being a hard-ass, but this was like the five millionth favor Wyatt had asked me for and he'd pretty much never done me any, so I was kind of tapped out in the favor department.

"Gretchen's morning sickness is too bad to go, and Mom and Dad have that wedding. You're the only option." I knew that, which both gave me leverage and also put a whole lot of pressure on my shoulders.

Wyatt smiled at me and changed tactics.

"I will pay you."

Ah, money. The ultimate incentive. Something that Wyatt could definitely use to get me to do what he wanted.

"How much?" I was going to need to know exact amounts, in writing, before even considering doing what he was asking.

He sighed for what seemed like forever and then wrote a number on his phone and showed it to me.

Wow. That was way more than I was expecting, but Wyatt always seemed to have money coming out his ass, despite never really working. We were both employees of our uncle's insurance agency, but he'd managed to get himself a cushy position with even cushier pay.

I looked around my mostly empty cabin and knew he had me. I needed the cash more than I needed my dignity.

Going from living under my parent's roof to being responsible for my own place had been a rude awakening and I was still scrambling to figure out how to make things work. Yes, I was renting the cabin from my family, but I still had to pay rent and utilities and that didn't even get into my student loans.

I sighed. "Okay. I'll do it."

Wyatt closed his eyes, and I could see he was relieved. Now he'd be in his fiancée's good graces. I still couldn't believe that he was getting fucking married. It was going to be a complete nightmare. Gretchen wanted it to happen before she had the baby for some reason, so we were all doing our best to plan the fastest, but most-elegant and social-media worthy, wedding she demanded. Just thinking about it gave me a migraine.

At least we still had a few months to go before that shitshow. Right now I was going to have to deal with the consequences of what I'd just agreed to do for Wyatt.

"All the hotels are booked, and so is the truck. We'll get your flight all set and I can drive you to the airport," he said. Wyatt was busy on his phone getting all the details settled.

"Are you going to tell her I'm coming?" I couldn't even say her name. I'd put her name in a box in my brain that I hadn't opened since high school. The phrase "she's dead to me" was an understatement.

"Yeah. Hold on a sec." He put one finger up and proceeded to call someone. By the tone of his voice when he said hello, it was Gretchen.

Ever since she'd gotten pregnant, Wyatt had gone from playboy to placater, and it was getting weird. I couldn't imagine what he was going to be like when that baby got here in six months.

Wyatt paced around my living room, using the softest tone I'd ever heard from him with Gretchen. I hoped she was grateful that I was helping her out of a jam. This was the favor to end all favors.

"I love you too, baby girl," Wyatt said, before hanging up.

Gross.

"Okay, we're good. Let me book your flight and I'll send you the details. I've got to go, Gretchen needs me." Another understatement.

"Okay," I said, waiting for him to thank me for this favor, but the gratitude didn't come. Didn't stop me from wishing for it as he slammed the door carelessly.

"So, I am going to Arizona in a few days," I said to Paige as we had dinner at the Pine State Bar and Grille. She was barely paying attention to me, too wrapped up in watching her girlfriend, Esme, tend bar.

"What?" she asked, looking up from her plate of wings. "You're doing what now?"

Her brown eyes were wide underneath her new bangs she'd gotten last week. The style made her look even more like a doll.

"I'm flying to Phoenix and driving a moving truck back with Gretchen's sister in it. For a week," I said.

"It doesn't take that long to get back from Phoenix, does it?" she asked, still glancing back and forth from me to Esme. Hopeless. Completely hopelessly in love.

I shook my head and stole one of her wings.

"No, but Gretchen had this whole sister road trip planned and they booked everything already, so I guess I'm going to be a stand-in sister." I tried not to gag.

Paige's mouth dropped open. "Holy shit, that's weird."

"Yes, it's going to be weird."

Another understatement to add to the list.

"Hey, can I get you another round?" Esme asked, leaning on the bar and winking at Paige.

"One more Paloma, please," Paige said, pushing her empty glass at Esme.

"You got it, baby," Esme said, and I couldn't help a little stab of jealousy as she and Paige looked at each other as if the other one hung the moon.

I *wanted* that. Paige had been trying to get me to try dating apps, but I just wasn't sure about them. I needed to do something, though. She had Esme, and my other closest friend, Linley, had her boyfriend, Gray. I was the fifth wheel and I hated it.

"Wait, weren't you and Natalie friends like a million years ago?" Paige asked, and I couldn't stop from cringing. I'd been kind of hoping she'd forgotten about that. Paige was a few years older than me, and we hadn't started hanging out until she started dating my brother. I thought she wouldn't remember what had happened when I was in middle school and she'd already been in high school.

"Yeah," I said, taking another wing. "Can I get an alcohol, please?" This was directed at Esme, who laughed. One of her favorite things to do was to mix up random mystery drinks and test them on us.

"I don't even care what it is," I said.

"You got it."

She did her thing and pushed a glass with brownish liquid in it toward me. I took a sip and savored as I swallowed. It tasted somehow like ginger ale and smoke and something else. Very nice.

"I like that," I said.

"Good to know," Esme said, slapping the bar and then moving on to take care of other patrons. The tourist season was still going strong, and things wouldn't start to calm down until at least October, when beach season gave way to leaf-peeping season.

"Here's to your weird week," Paige said, holding up her glass. I tapped it with mine.

"Let's get weird."

I honestly had no idea what to pack, so I just kind of sprinkled in a little bit of everything. I definitely didn't want to get stranded without something I needed. I'd already gotten the week off work, so that was set, and all I had to do now was get up at the ass-crack of dawn so Wyatt could drive me to the airport. He still hadn't thanked me, and neither had Gretchen. She was too busy with her first of many maternity photo shoots. Seriously, she was barely even showing, but did that matter? No. This was going to be the longest pregnancy in the history of time, and we hadn't even gotten to the baby showers yet. Yes, she was planning multiple showers. The count was up to three already.

If only Natalie wasn't involved, I would have loved to take a whole week to get away from my family and my boring ass job. But no, I couldn't have a simple vacation. It had to be complicated and involve the girl who was once my best friend.

Not that I was still bitter about it or anything. It was fine, whatever. I just hoped she appreciated what I was doing for her.

I hated that I knew the reason Natalie didn't drive was because of anxiety. She'd tried to do driver's ed with the rest of our class and had such a bad panic attack during the first session that the entire school had been talking about it for weeks.

We hadn't been talking then, but I'd still wanted to reach out to her and tell her it was okay. It had taken years to destroy that impulse.

Wyatt was on the phone with Gretchen nearly the entire drive to the airport. Having to listen to what should be a private conversation while you were trapped in a metal box was a special kind of torture.

It was a relief to haul my carryon out of the trunk and

wave goodbye to him. We weren't huggers. At least he remembered to tell me to call him when I got to Arizona.

It wasn't a direct flight, so I had to do some running to get to my gate for my second flight, but other than that, things went relatively smooth. No nosy seatmates, no one putting their nasty feet on my armrest. I slept most of the way.

When I landed in Phoenix around lunchtime, I was hungry and grumpy and wishing I could jump forward in time a week. I still had to go get the rental truck, figure out how to drive it, and then make it to Natalie's apartment in one piece. Thankfully, Gretchen had hired people to help pack the truck, so my services weren't required for that, and I had a hotel booked for that night since Natalie lived in a one-bedroom and there was just no fucking way.

As I waited for the car I'd called to take me to pick up the rental truck, a text message from an unknown number came in. I figured it was just a mistake text, but then I read it.

Hey, thanks for coming.

My breath caught in my chest.

This is Natalie, btw

Oh.

Wyatt had neglected to give me her number, but someone had given her mine.

I knew I needed to respond, but I didn't know how, so I just got in the taxi and confirmed with the driver the address of the truck rental place. I sat in the backseat, trying to figure out what to say to someone I hadn't talked to in so many years.

Just going to get the truck. Be there soon.

There. That wasn't too awkward, I hoped. Just a simple exchange of details.

We were just two people, coordinating a cross-country move.

Acknowledgments

I can't believe this is the first book I'm releasing in 2021. Let's just say a worldwide pandemic is not super conducive to writing sweet summer romances, but I got it done! It was so nice to get lost in Paige's pansexual hijinks. I hope this book is as much of a mental vacation for you as it has been for me.

Firstly, I have to thank my editor and friend, Laura Helseth, who's always like WHEN ARE YOU SENDING ME THE NEXT BOOK? and who will say "sure" when I ask "Can you edit a book this week?" with zero notice. I don't know what I'd do without you!

The past year and a half has been lonely as hell, and I've seriously leaned on my writer community so much. I always want to mention names (and I have before), but I'm always so worried about leaving anyone out. So, if you're a writer, and we've interacted, consider yourself thanked!

It's strange reflecting on this year, because it's officially five years since I released Style, my first f/f book. That was also my first out Pride. I was still so unsure and finding labels and wondering if I was "queer enough" to write a queer book. Five years on and I'm not worried about being queer enough. I almost wish I could go back and tell my past self that they ARE queer enough and to stop caring what random strangers on the internet think about their labels and so forth. All this is to say, if you're worried if you're "enough," I'm here to tell you: yes. You are.

About the Author

Chelsea M. Cameron is a New York Times/USA Today/Internationally Bestselling author from Maine who now lives and works in Boston. She's a red velvet cake enthusiast, obsessive tea drinker, former cheerleader, and world's worst video gamer. When not writing, she enjoys watching infomercials, eating brunch in bed, tweeting, and playing fetch with her cat, Sassenach. She has a degree in journalism from the University of Maine, Orono that she promptly abandoned to write about the people in her own head. More often than not, these people turn out to be just as weird as she is.

Connect with her on Twitter, Facebook, Instagram, Bookbub, Goodreads, and her website.

If you liked this book, please take a few moments to **leave a review**. Authors really appreciate this and it helps new readers find books they might enjoy. Thank you!

Also by Chelsea M. Cameron

The Noctalis Chronicles

Fall and Rise Series

My Favorite Mistake Series

The Surrender Saga

Rules of Love Series

UnWritten

Behind Your Back Series

OTP Series

Brooks (The Benson Brothers)

The Violet Hill Series

Unveiled Attraction

Anyone but You

Didn't Stay in Vegas

Wicked Sweet

Christmas Inn Maine

Bring Her On

The Girl Next Door

Who We Could Be

Castleton Hearts

Mainely Books Club

Love in Vacationland

9133276SR00134